The Landscape of
King Arthur

GEOFFREY ASHE

The Landscape of
King Arthur

GEOFFREY ASHE

Webb & Bower

MICHAEL JOSEPH

Frontispiece
A view from the Mote of Mark across the Rough Firth

First published in Great Britain 1987 by
Webb & Bower (Publishers) Limited
9 Colleton Crescent, Exeter, Devon EX2 4BY
in association with Michael Joseph Limited
27 Wright's Lane, London W8 5TZ

Designed by Vic Giolitto

Production by Nick Facer/Rob Kendrew

Text Copyright © 1987 Webb & Bower (Publishers) Limited

Illustrations Copyright 1987 © Webb & Bower/Simon McBride

British Library Cataloguing in Publication Data

Ashe, Geoffrey
    The landscape of King Arthur.
    1. Arthur, *King*   2. Europe ———
    Description and travel ——— 1971–
    I. Title   II. McBride, Simon
    914   DA152.5.A7
    ISBN 0-86350-168-0

Typeset in Great Britain by August Filmsetting,
Haydock, St Helens.

Printed and bound in Portugal by
Printer Portuguesa

Contents

Introduction

How did i first encounter King Arthur? I'm not sure. It may have been in a book of legends for children that included several Arthurian tales, suitably adapted. But all I remember of them in that setting is a colour plate reproducing a Victorian painting of Sir Galahad on his knees before the Holy Grail, which hovered in the air all aglow and looking like an awkwardly large athletic trophy. The scene didn't particularly impress me.

When slightly older I was a devoted reader of Richmal Crompton's 'William' stories. In one of these, the eleven-year-old William forms the Knights of the Square Table and puts up an advertisement saying wrongs righted (probably misspelt, but alas, I no longer have the book to check). By the time I read that story I certainly knew somehow or other what William was thinking of. Later again I recall a teacher of English who, every so often, used to recite a passage from Tennyson's *Morte d'Arthur*—'The old order changeth, yielding place to new' (etc, etc.)—but never seemed to branch out from it.

There was much journeying in my life, because my father was general manager of a travel agency. Did we go to Tintagel or any other Arthurian places? I don't know. One or two postcards in old albums suggest that we did. If so, they made no impression. At Penzance my mother told me of the sunken land of Lyonesse, and the church bells heard ringing under water, but if she said anything about Tristan, that too made no impression.

A time came when I read more. I read Tennyson's *Idylls of the King*, or some of them, and those two great medieval Arthurians Geoffrey of Monmouth and Sir Thomas Malory. I became familiar with the main characters and topics of Arthurian lore: Arthur himself and Guinevere, Merlin and Lancelot, the Round Table and Camelot and the Grail Quest, all in resplendent imagery. Yet it still didn't register, somehow. I realized that this was a major body of literature, parts of it powerful and memorable if other parts were decidedly less so. But genuine interest came only with a growing awareness that the whole thing was, in a sense, an optical illusion. It was valid on its own level, of course. No one could quarrel with readers or film-goers who were content with that, and saw no reason to look beyond. Yet, to quote Bernard Shaw in a very different connection, there *was* a beyond. There was more to it than met the eye.

After all, King Arthur hadn't actually reigned in the Middle Ages. History books didn't recognize him or leave any room for him. The medieval trappings, the medieval themes of chivalry, courtly love and so forth, were only a garb in which medieval story-tellers had dressed up the Legend. Quite early I was vaguely conscious that Arthur really belonged somewhere else—or nowhere at all—or in an undatable realm of myth. For one thing, he wasn't even English. He was a Celtic Briton, a sort of proto-Welshman. That put him in an antiquity that stretched backwards into mist. Malory pulled me up sharply with his sudden exactitude in a throw-away line, to the effect that the Grail Quest began 454 years after the Passion of Christ. That meant the 480s AD. But, for goodness' sake! I'd been taught that in those decades after the end of Roman Britain, the Britons were all being massacred by invading Saxons or driven into remote mountain refuges, so how could Arthur's kingdom fit in? Not till long after did I learn that my school history books had been wronger here than legend.

I have a notion that, at some stage, I supposed Arthur could be linked with Atlantis. Even that plunge into a fabulous past was not wholly ridiculous. Whatever might be the case with Arthur himself, Merlin was reputed to have put up Stonehenge, and C.S. Lewis wrote of the magician's Atlantean quality in his science-fiction novel *That Hideous Strength*. Eventually I felt that William Blake hit it, if cryptically, when he made Arthur a human being mythified, one who absorbed a whole symbolism of Britain, covering many centuries: 'The Giant Albion was Patriarch of the Atlantic . . . one of those the Greeks called Titans. The stories of Arthur are the acts of Albion, applied to a Prince of the fifth century.' By the time I discovered Blake, British legend had finally begun coming to life for me. But it had only done so, it had only begun to root itself and take substance, when I brought it down to earth at a specific place.

Or rather, when someone brought it down for me, in Ottawa during the Second World War. My job gave me access to Canada's parliamentary library, which housed many volumes not often in demand from the members. At that time I was discovering several authors and books that were to mean a great deal to me. Outstanding among the authors was G.K. Chesterton, and outstanding among the books was his *Short History of England*, which he wrote in 1917. This is not really a history but a series of Chestertonian essays, and despite several early reprints it is not one of his best-remembered works. Excerpts appeared in a 1985 Chesterton anthology, but not the passages that stirred my imagination. They come in a chapter headed 'The Age of Legends'.

The past is always present: yet it is not what was, but whatever seems to have been . . . . It is therefore very practical to put in a few words, if possible, something of what a man of these islands in the Dark Ages would have said about his ancestors and his inheritance. I will attempt here to put some of the simpler things in their order of importance as he would have seen them; and if we are to understand our fathers who first made this country anything like itself, it is most important that we should remember that if this was not their real past, it was their real memory . . .

[After the Crucifixion] St Joseph of Arimathea, one of the few followers of the new religion who seem to have been wealthy, set sail as a missionary, and after long voyages came to that litter of little islands which seemed to the men of the Mediterranean something like the last clouds of sunset. He came upon the western and wilder side of that wild and western land, and made his way to a valley which through all the oldest records is called Avalon . . . Here the pilgrim planted his staff in the soil; and it took root as a tree that blossoms on Christmas Day . . .

All who took their mission from the divine tragedy bore tangible fragments which became the germs of churches and cities. St Joseph carried the cup which held the wine of the Last Supper and the blood of the Crucifixion to that shrine in Avalon which we now call Glastonbury; and it became the heart of a whole universe of legends and romances, not only for Britain but for Europe. Throughout this tremendous and branching tradition it is called the Holy Grail. The vision of it was especially the reward of that ring of powerful paladins whom King Arthur feasted at a Round Table, a symbol of heroic comradeship such as was afterwards imitated or invented by medieval knighthood.

Much further on, Chesterton has this to say about the Puritans who beheaded Charles I:

It was, properly considered, but a very secondary example of their strange and violent simplicity that one of them, before a mighty mob at Whitehall, cut off the anointed head . . . . For another, far away in the western shires, cut down the thorn of Glastonbury, from which had grown the whole story of Britain.

After reading this I looked up Glastonbury, and its legends of Joseph and the Grail and Arthur, in an encyclopedia. It appeared that Chesterton was reading back medieval and even post-medieval beliefs into the so-called Dark Ages long before, when they had not yet taken shape. I know now that beliefs ancestral to them probably had done so, and not without a factual foundation. But I was not much affected by what the encyclopedia told me, and would not have been much affected, either, if I had known then what has come to light since. Chesterton's vision was what mattered. It was henceforth certain that when I returned to England, I would sooner or later go to Somerset and take a look at Glastonbury.

The way it happened was strange. During a stay in Devonshire, I noticed a bus station advertising a day excursion taking in Glastonbury, Wells, and Weston-super-Mare. This was it. My wife and I boarded the bus. It crossed the counties, it traversed the Somerset levels, it approached Glastonbury with its arresting hill-cluster and tower-surmounted Tor. Expectation rose high as the bus entered the town. It approached the ancient Abbey and passed it and... didn't stop. I had a fleeting glimpse of grey stone ruins, and then the bus turned up the High Street and whirled out of Glastonbury on the far side. It did stop in Wells. While I have nothing against Wells, the length of that stop seemed inordinate.

Such an omission would be unusual now. The attitudes of people in Britain to their own past are apt to fluctuate, but the modern rebirth of interest in Glastonbury is not, I would say, reversible. Today the tours do stop.

Even seen so frustratingly, even without true contact, the place struck me as extraordinary. Yet I was not moved to pay it a proper visit, or explore its history and mythology further, till seven years later, and for a second time the impulse came to me from a book in a Canadian library. To be precise, the Public Library of Toronto. Having been reminded of Glastonbury, I went to see what it had on the subject. It turned out to have a surprising amount, including some highly uncommon items. Among these was *Glastonbury and England*, the little-known first book of Christopher Hollis, historian and politician, a writer of a younger generation than Chesterton, but under similar influences. Hollis had much to say of the real glories of Glastonbury Abbey as well as its legendary background. He spoke of its dissolution and desolation at the hands of Henry VIII, and ended by quoting the death-bed prophecy of Austin Ringwode, the last survivor of the community, said to have lived on in a cottage in the neighbourhood till 1587: 'The Abbey will one day be repaired and rebuilt for the like worship which has ceased; and then peace and plenty will for a long time abound.'

That moved me more specifically than Chesterton had. No matter whether Austin Ringwode really had paranormal knowledge. A prophecy could create its own fulfilment. Glastonbury was no mere heap of dead ruins, it was alive. So I saw it, and while the Abbey has not been rebuilt, many events have borne out my general conviction—pilgrimages, festivals, the growth of an international reputation, and much else.

Here too, though, my experience was strange. I began writing a book on Glastonbury, and in the course of reading already-existing books, I never found another that mentioned the prophecy. Where had Hollis got hold of it? I asked him, and he told me where he thought he had, but his recollection turned out to be at fault. I asked Aelred Watkin, sometime headmaster of

Downside, a leading authority on the Abbey. He told me the prophecy was mentioned in a nineteenth-century magazine and couldn't be traced back further, and Austin Ringwode was a figure of doubtful authenticity, unidentifiable in Abbey records. Only Hollis among modern historians had picked up this dubious item, and Hollis's book itself was rare. During my researches I never came across it in any other place, apart from the British Museum. Not only had inspiration struck in Toronto Public Library, it would probably not have struck anywhere else, because other libraries that I might have frequented didn't possess the unique book. Furthermore, it depended on something which might well be a figment of romantic imagination.

Nevertheless, the thing had happened and I was involved, and perhaps now after many years I can offer a guess as to who Austin Ringwode was... more of that presently. My own book appeared, with the title *King Arthur's Avalon*. Arthur himself was not the primary interest. But my discussion of him, reflecting historical speculations which I had studied along the way, attracted the interest of the public. I went on from there.

Glastonbury

1 St Benedict's Church

2 St Mary's Church

3 Abbot's Kitchen

4 Assembly Rooms

5 Tribunal

6 St John's Church

7 Abbey House

8 Abbey Barn

9 St Michael's Chapel (remains)

10 Abbey Ruins

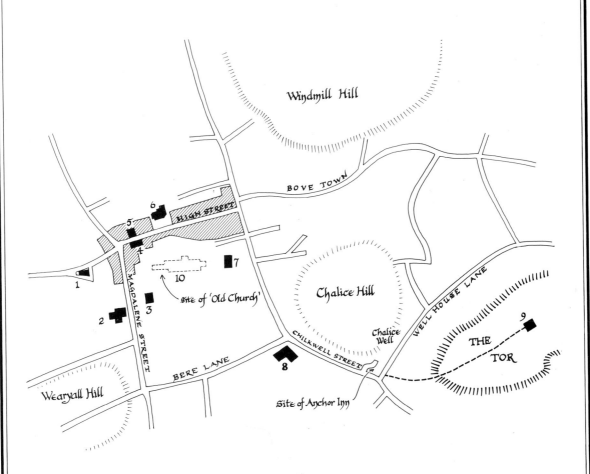

1. Beginning at Glastonbury

W HEN YOU CONFRONT THIS PLACE, cradled in the hill-cluster known as the Isle of Avalon, you confront a long history and a renowned mythology. You also confront uncertainties as to how much of the latter actually *is* mythology in any authentic sense. Glastonbury's mysterious alive-ness is shown in its capacity for continued myth-making. As Aelred Watkin put it to me: 'You have only to tell some crazy story in Glastonbury, and in ten years' time it's an ancient Somerset legend.' True, how true! The place not only creates mythology, it attracts people who aid and abet the process. It harbours every kind of eccentric, guru and fringe mystic, some of them wise and well-disposed, some... not. When guiding visitors, I often tell them they are in the Los Angeles of England. I live, myself, in a house that once belonged to a magician. She wrote and taught under the name Dion Fortune, and made her home into an esoteric hostel. Her mortal remains repose in the town cemetery.

The Glastonbury landscape is weird. With those words I opened *King Arthur's Avalon.* The surrounding country is low, formerly an expanse of marsh and open water, still criss-crossed with drainage channels. When you stand on high ground and look out over it, hills in the distance play tricks with the perspective. A frequent visitor, the Swedish-born artist Monica Sjöö, has written of 'distortions', of 'not being able to locate yourself in space', and a consequent 'feeling of the fantastic'. Fay Weldon, the novelist, has had somewhat similar reactions. Pomparles Bridge over the Brue between Glastonbury and its neighbour town, shoe-dominated Street, is the place where Arthur's sword was cast away into the water. Never mind that it was cast away at four other places, two in Cornwall and two in Wales. Pomparles Bridge, at any relevant date, would have provided a stretch of water to cast it into, and even now, after heavy rain, a shallow lake a mile or two long can reappear covering the meadows.

Glastonbury itself is a town of seven or eight thousand, and I hasten to add that most of its permanent inhabitants are thoroughly sane. Hides and fleeces have long been the raw materials of its industry. The Avalonian hill-cluster in which it lies was once quite close to being an actual island. The hills composing this are all different shapes. Windmill Hill is a modest rise covered with a housing development. Wearyall Hill—properly Wirral, but locally Wearyall, for a reason which I shall tell—is a long ridge rising to a bulbous end. Chalice Hill is a soft rounded dome. East of it, with a little valley between, is the surprising whale-back of the Tor, with a ruined tower on top, 518 feet above sea-level.

On the Tor, and in the valley, and among the Abbey ruins in the angle of the main streets, you catch echoes of the story of Arthur. The Abbey, indeed, claimed to have his grave. But even if you take these tales at face value they don't carry you back to the beginnings. In the last centuries before Christ, Celts or Ancient Britons or whatever you like to call them were leading a fairly sophisticated life in two 'lake-villages' at nearby Godney and Meare, built on artificial islets above the marshes and flood-waters. A rich archaeological haul from those villages is in the town museum in the High Street.

GLASTONBURY TOR

In another spot too, closer to the heart of the place, human frequentation goes back a long way.

The Tor is . . . well, atmospheric. I have known would-be climbers who, though healthy in body, were psychologically powerless to face the ascent. From Dion Fortune's house, on the lower slope, you can look up through the back windows and watch the sun and moon emerging from behind the Tor in a golden or pearly glow. Normally the surface is green, but in the drought of 1976 it was brown, and the occasional winter of heavy snow turns it white. Sometimes, when all below is blanketed with autumnal mist, the summit rises into clear sky and sunshine, and a climber who stands there floats above the mist on an aerial platform.

There is nothing obscure about the name. 'Tor' is simply an old West-country word for a hill. The Tor's appearance, however, is a bewilderment. A question asked by numerous visitors is whether it is artificial. From some angles it looks like a kind of stepped pyramid. Actually, it is a natural form-ation, but artificially shaped. All around it run mysterious paths or terraces, sometimes sharply vivid in light and shade, sometimes distinguishable by changes in the grass colour. Those who want to dispel the mystery are apt to tell you that there is an obvious common-sense explanation for them. The trouble is that you will hear half a dozen such explanations, all contradicting each other. Which means, in practice, that there isn't one.

Dinas Bran. Ruins inside an earthwork system above the Welsh town of Llangollen, in an area with Arthurian associations. Llangollen takes its name from a church of St Collen, who is said to have gone to Glastonbury and encountered strange beings on the Tor.

A favoured notion that they are lynchets, formed by and for medieval agriculture, is correct to the extent that a small part of the system was used and developed in this way, but certainly comes nowhere near explaining it as a whole. Some of the would-be de-mystifiers assert that there is nothing special about the Tor, and other hills are terraced similarly, but this is quite simply wrong. As for dating, the terraces existed in the seventeenth century and there can be no serious doubt that they are much older. A medieval allusion to encircling woods might, on the face of it, suggest that they must have been made after a subsequent clearance. But all the probabilities are that the woods were confined to the lower slopes and that the steep mass of the Tor proper rose above into the open, complete with its terracing.

Dion Fortune, who cherished the engaging belief that colonists from Atlantis lived hereabouts, suggested that the terraces were remnants of a ritual pathway thousands of years old, spiralling up the hill. She never worked out this idea. In the 1960s an Irishman, Geoffrey Russell, did—up to a point. He claimed that they formed a complex labyrinthine pattern of immense age, a backtracking septenary spiral, which turns up also in Crete and Italy and Ireland and elsewhere, and is carved on a rock near Tintagel, Arthur's reputed Cornish birthplace.

Russell made models to show how the Tor maze would work. In general he presented his case rather confusingly and failed to persuade archaeologists at the National Trust, which owns the Tor. Philip Rahtz, however, who excavated the summit area in 1964–6, was prepared to take the idea seriously, and in his book *Invitation to Archaeology* he reaffirms his willingness, adding that Russell's models 'look quite convincing'.

In 1979 I tested the theory myself, walking along the terraces, round and round the Tor on a hot afternoon, to see whether the maze-pattern would fit. I concluded that it did and I think so still. Explain it as you please. But the mere *possibility* of tracing it seems to me to banish all 'obvious common-sense explanations'. How many hills are there, anywhere, on which you could do that? And what are the odds against that complicated, perhaps unique possibility occurring by accident at Glastonbury of all places? In Professor Rahtz's view, if the maze is real, it probably dates from the Neolithic age of Stonehenge and Avebury and other vast ritual works, in the second or third millennium BC. The people who carried out those works were far earlier than the Celts, who imagined that they must have been giants. Out of that fancy grew a story that they built Stonehenge itself in Ireland, and that it took the arts of Merlin to transplant it to Salisbury Plain.

Whatever the truth about the maze on the Tor, it is a fact that mazes used to be linked with beliefs about the Underworld; and it is also a fact that the Tor is spoken of in legend as hollow, an Underworld point of entry. One story tells of the wandering Welsh holy man St Collen. He lived in some ill-recorded time, the sixth century perhaps. Llangollen in North Wales takes its name from a church dedicated to him. (You may wonder about the *g*. Letters in Welsh words change according to rules which foreigners, among them Prince Charles, have confessed to finding difficult.) Collen, it is said, wandered as far as Somerset and lived for a while as a hermit on Glastonbury Tor, in 'a cell under a rock, in a secret place out of the way'. The Tor has few rocks, and the likeliest one is on the south side. A hermit could dig out a nook behind it, if not exactly get under it. The spot is interesting because it plays a part in the maze theory, and might have been regarded as magical.

Anyhow, one day Collen heard two men talking outside his cell. They said the Tor was the home of Gwyn ap Nudd, king of the fairy-folk and lord of Annwfn, as the Welsh called the Underworld. Collen put his head out and told them Gwyn and his fairy-folk were demons. They replied that this was an insult and he would have to meet Gwyn and answer for it. Not long after, a messenger arrived summoning Collen to the top for the encounter. He refused, but Gwyn's summons was repeated on several successive days, with threats, until at last he consented and made the climb, taking a flask of holy water.

Entering the hill through a magical opening, he found himself in a palace. King Gwyn, seated on a golden chair, offered him food, but Collen knew better than to accept it. Gwyn gestured at his retainers, inviting Collen to admire their red and blue liveries. Collen replied: 'Their dress is good of its kind, but the red is the red of fire and the blue is the blue of cold.' He scattered his holy water, the palace vanished, and the saint was alone on the hilltop. (Gwyn, by the way, appears with Arthur in a Welsh tale, and is reputed to emerge from the realm of Faerie to ride with him through the clouds.)

Kindred beliefs about the Tor being hollow are on record in the reign of Elizabeth I and in modern times. To this day you can hear local tales of a chamber below the summit, or a well sinking far into the depths, or a tunnel running all the way to the Abbey, a distance of more than half a mile. Rash explorers are supposed to have found a way in and to have come out insane. Dowsers have claimed to detect a network of subterranean waterways, and I have even heard of an underground lake, perhaps with the Lady of the Lake in it.

A lingering medieval sense of the Tor's uncanniness may have left its mark on the church at the top, of which only the empty tower remains. The monks who built it dedicated it to St Michael, archangelic conqueror of the infernal powers. He would have been a suitable person to hold them down. The odd thing is that a previous church of Michael on the same site collapsed in an earthquake, a disaster so rare in England that one might be excused for wondering whether the infernal powers were entirely suppressed.

But to return to facts. In 1964–6, as I said, Philip Rahtz excavated the topmost area. He found traces of human activity in prehistoric times, and of fair-sized buildings and continuous settlement during the sixth century AD, originating perhaps a little earlier. Wine-drinking, meat-eating and metal-working were apparent. A local chief may have had a fort up there. That possibility could be linked with the oldest known story bringing Arthur to Glastonbury. It was set down about 1130 by a Welsh monk, Caradoc of Llancarfan. He was writing the life of Gildas, another cleric who flourished six centuries earlier and who was the author of a maddeningly uninformative tract that might have given us the truth about Arthur, but doesn't. Gildas, according to Caradoc, lived during the last phase of his career at the Glastonbury monastery. A sentence in Gildas's own book suggests that he did at least know of it, conceivably at first hand. While he was there (says Caradoc), Melwas, the ruler of Somerset, carried off Arthur's wife 'Guennuvar'— Guinevere, of course; most of these names have a variety of spellings—and kept her at Glastonbury. Arthur assembled troops from Devon and Cornwall to recover her, but the watery surroundings made it difficult. Gildas and the abbot mediated, and the dispute was settled by negotiation, the lady being restored.

Did that fort on top of the Tor (if it was a fort) belong to Melwas? A bleak place to take Guinevere, but, in Professor Rahtz's opinion, it would have been only an outpost of a larger complex. Its date is fairly close to a credible time for Arthur, close enough to make Caradoc's tale look fairly well invented, if hardly historical. Who knows? The theme of the Queen's abduction is taken up by medieval romancers with embroideries and variations, but Glastonbury is where it starts. Caradoc mentions a belief that the place's old Celtic name was Ynys-witrin, the Isle of Glass. This has been explained as a mistake due to a popular supposition that the first syllable of the English name is literally 'glass'. The whole etymological question is a nightmare tangle which I prefer not to get involved in. But in Celtic eyes a Glass Island, especially one with such an eerie hill on it, would have been enchanted ground.

THE ZODIAC

One way or another, Glastonbury does seem to have been a sacred spot before Christianity. Even the tale of Melwas has a pagan air, recalling mythical abductions like that of Persephone among the Greeks; and when romancers adapt the story, that impression grows stronger if anything. Glastonbury's pre-Christian aura is easily felt, yet hard to be precise about. The Tor maze, if accepted, is a clue. I suspect that some of the other modern notions are really attempts to find a basis for the feeling.

The best known of these speculations concerns the Glastonbury Zodiac, which supposedly covers a large part of the landscape overlooked by the Tor. It was first expounded in the inter-war period by a lady named Katharine Maltwood, and has since been re-expounded in exuberant detail by Mary Caine. What is asserted is that central Somerset has gigantic signs of the Zodiac marked out on it. Formed by a miscellany of physical features, they are arranged in a rough circle ten miles across. Mrs Maltwood called this the Temple of the Stars. Glastonbury Tor is part of Aquarius. Clues are said to occur in a medieval romance, *Perlesvaus*. Indeed, the Arthurian Legend itself is alleged to have its roots in this Zodiac. It is the true Round Table. Sagittarius, the Archer, is a mounted man interpreted as Arthur himself.

These signs, we are assured, are visible from the air. In a sense I dare say they are, if the person who flies over them is a believer and knows in advance which features to pick out. The trouble is that the landscape lends itself to this sort of thing, as you can see if you look at a large-scale map. Zodiac-finders don't compose the figures out of features of a single type. They bring in hills, rivers, hedges, roads, drainage ditches, all kinds of things. By picking out a different set of hills, etc., it is not very difficult to compose other figures equally good. I've seen it done. And even with all the licence they allow themselves, they can't get the Zodiac right. They have to settle for a ship instead of a crab, a dove instead of a pair of scales, a unicorn instead of a goat, a phoenix instead of a water-carrier, and claim that these are traditional variants on the signs we know.

Katharine Maltwood believed that the Zodiac was laid out around 2700 BC, before the flooding of the Somerset levels. But if so—and for that matter, if the Zodiac is much more recent—one is bound to ask what was the point of laying it out, when nobody could take to the air to see it. Furthermore, most of the features that allegedly form it (roads, for instance) were not there thousands of years ago. The current retort to this is that a divine earth-force was at work creating a Zodiac, and human beings were unconsciously impelled to make roads and so forth in obedience to its promptings.

All objections would have to yield if the signs were visibly there. I don't think they are. I have studied aerial photographs, and I know what the Zodiac-finders expect me to see, and I don't see it. Twice I have invited them to show the photos to people unfamiliar with the theory, and ask what they do see. The challenge has never been taken up. Still, I would not impugn the Zodiac-finders' good faith. They look, and they see. I can only count this as a conspicuous instance of Glastonbury's spell-weaving.

One question which is not altogether futile is whether anybody conceived the same idea, or something like it, before Mrs Maltwood. John Dee, a learned astrologer in the reign of Elizabeth I, took an interest in Glastonbury and is said to have spoken of zodiacal earthworks, but there seems to be no proof. However, his older contemporary Nostradamus, a more notorious astrologer, alluded to England as 'the land of the great heavenly temple', in lines that have been held to glance at events in Somerset. His phrase is not unlike Mrs Maltwood's 'Temple of the Stars'.

CHALICE WELL

In the valley between the Tor and Chalice Hill is a long, narrow and charming garden. This is the domain of the Chalice Well Trust. Chalice Well is a spring, enclosed since the Middle Ages in stonework. It gives a name to the road running along the valley, Well House Lane. The flow of water has never failed, even in the severest droughts. Its source is unknown. A slight iron impregnation gives a distinctive orange stain to the stones over which it runs. After it has trickled down through the garden, concealed piping carries it off. In 1750 a certain Matthew Chancellor dreamed that if he drank the water on seven successive Sunday mornings his asthma would be cured. He did, and it was. Glastonbury became a spa briefly rivalling Bath, and blindness, deafness and ulcers were also reported to be cured; but after a year or two someone drank too much and died, and the vogue blew over.

'Chalice' is a form of the well's name prompted by literary imagination. It used to be called Chalk Well, 'chalk' being used in an old sense to mean limestone. Its real name survives in nearby Chilkwell Street. But the reddish tinge in the water caused it to be known also as the Blood Spring, and eventually someone hit on the idea that the Holy Grail, the chalice of Christ, in which Joseph of Arimathea caught drops of the Saviour's blood, lay somewhere in the depths. In which case it must be confessed that Arthur's knights who rode out in quest of it were all wasting their time.

Here we confront an important branch of the Arthurian Legend, the one Chesterton emphasized. Joseph appears briefly in the Gospels as a wealthy member of the Jewish council in Jerusalem, secretly a disciple of Christ, who obtained his body from Pilate after the Crucifixion and laid it in the tomb. In the twelfth century—possibly before, but documentation fails—non-scriptural writings began to tell how the hallowed vessel of the Last Supper had come into his possession and been conveyed to Britain and to the 'Vales of Avalon'. At first it was not agreed whether he made the journey in person. Friends and relatives of his, under divine guidance, might have been responsible. But presently Joseph was said to have come over, to have entrusted the Grail to custodians, to have built the first church in the Glastonbury Abbey precinct, to have settled as a hermit with a group of companions. Long afterwards, in Arthur's time, the Grail had receded into a realm of mystery, and many knights of the Round Table undertook the quest. It had wonder-working powers and conferred a supreme spiritual experience on whoever was worthy. Several knights saw it, but only Galahad attained the full vision.

Let me make it clear, in passing, that to put the matter thus is to simplify greatly. The Grail stories are full of strange incidents and imagery giving tantalizing glimpses of pre-Christian myth, perhaps even ritual, such as Glastonbury offers in other ways. The Grail makes its literary début before Joseph does, and its nature is not at first explained. But the subject is too big to pursue now.

Chalice Well enthusiasts claim that Joseph and his companions did truly come to Britain, and settled in this part of the Isle, not, as the monks maintained, on the future site of the Abbey. Much else is claimed about spiritual presences and mystic powers. Dion Fortune, the magician in whose house I live, wrote of Chalice Well as 'the wonderful holy well of St Joseph and Merlin and the Graal'. Medieval authors give no support to the idea that the chalice was thought to be at the bottom of it. Yet the enthusiasts are not on a totally false trail. The well may have been a sacred spring before Christianity, and in the Christian era there are interesting written traditions, even though they do not say what the Chalice Well folk say.

One Arthurian romancer, the anonymous author of *Perlesvaus* or *The High History of the Holy Grail* (the book where Mrs Maltwood found hints for her Zodiac), says he did research at a monastery in Avalon. He certainly means Glastonbury, and he describes a visit to the place by Sir Lancelot. Lancelot rides uphill, sees a spring and a chapel, and meets hermits. Scholars have ridiculed the author and accused him of lying, because his description doesn't fit the site of the Abbey, and therefore he plainly didn't know Glastonbury. The trouble with such scholars is their reluctance to go and look. I discovered years ago that if you approach the Tor area by way of Cinnamon Lane, the old road which Lancelot would have taken, the description fits very neatly. Whoever wrote this romance did know what he was talking about. His spring is the one that now feeds Chalice Well, and he portrays hermits living near it in Arthur's time.

Towards the close of Malory's Arthurian work, we are told that Lancelot and other survivors went to dwell as hermits in a valley near Glastonbury between two hills. Here again we are surely glimpsing that little valley with Chalice Well in it. Here is the same tradition as in *Perlesvaus*. At the foot of the Chalice Well property, beside Chilkwell Street, there used to be an old inn called the Anchor Inn, while the nearby orchard on the Tor's lower slope, where Dion Fortune put her house, was formerly Anchor Orchard. A ship's anchor would make little sense. The reference is to anchorites, hermits. They may or may not have actually lived here in early times; they were undoubtedly believed to have done so, long before the Chalice Well Trust voiced a similar belief, and we shall see further evidence for this in its place.

THE THORN

Best known of the Joseph legends, probably, is the one about the Holy Thorn. Its locale is another of the hills, the ridge of Wirral, from which you can look beyond towards the Bristol Channel, and back towards the Tor and the town. In the Zodiac theory it forms one of the Fishes. The reason for the popular change from Wirral to Wearyall is that Joseph and his party are said to have arrived by boat and disembarked here. Having traversed thousands of miles from Palestine, they were *weary all*. Joseph drove his staff into the earth and it miraculously became a tree, the Glastonbury Thorn, blossoming at Christmas.

Glastonbury. Wearyall Hill, where according to legend Joseph of Arimathea and his companions first set foot in the Isle of Avalon, and Joseph planted his staff which blossomed as the Holy Thorn. The original tree, cut down by a Puritan, has many descendants. Wearyall's present specimen was planted in 1951.

While the actual story of Joseph's staff is not very old, the tree on Wearyall Hill was real enough, and was viewed with reverence in the later Middle Ages. It did blossom at Christmas, approximately. As Chesterton recalled, a Puritan later cut it down, in the belief that the reverence for it was superstitious. However, it left plenty of descendants. In 1752, when England adopted the reformed calendar involving a shift of eleven days, crowds gathered at Glastonbury to watch what the trees would do. They failed to make the adjustment. However, the small white winter blossoms do appear more or less in the Christmas season, depending on the weather. Cuttings from the tree in front of St John's Church, in the High Street, are sent to the reigning sovereign. A specimen back on Wearyall Hill was planted in 1951 on the reputed site of the original, marked, though perhaps erroneously, by a stone slab.

Joseph's advent by water is at least plausibly imagined. Wharves of the Roman era have been identified on the banks of the Brue, one of them near the tip of Wearyall. As for the Thorn, it is not an English type. The ancestral tree was either a freak or of East Mediterranean provenance. A pilgrim or crusader may have brought it from the right general area. One of its descendants is outside the Episcopalian cathedral in Washington, DC, where, some years ago, a cutting from it was shown to a government tree expert without explanation, and he pronounced it to be Syrian. More recently, when Prince Charles and Princess Diana were in Washington, a local interviewee alleged that the Thorn outside the cathedral was reputed to blossom when British royalty visited the United States. Glastonbury's myth-making powers extend a long way.

THE ABBEY

In Glastonbury during the Middle Ages, Joseph was viewed chiefly as the Abbey's founder, or, at least, as the first Christian on the site. He was not stressed very much until a late phase, but a story of his advent was chronicled and improved upon. It was not the same as the tale told by Grail romancers; for one thing, it had no Grail in it. But the notion of his coming to Britain at all is so outlandish that many have found it hard to dismiss as pure fancy. He is a grotesquely unlikely person to think of as acquiring the Grail, since he was not present at the Last Supper; or as going on a British mission, since he is never spoken of, even in apocryphal legend, as a traveller to such remote parts. If some medieval fantasist wanted to bring a biblical character to Britain, far more impressive candidates were ready to hand. Legend had long spoken of missions by St Paul, St Peter, and others. Yet they were passed over, and the wellnigh-incredible Joseph won out.

Therefore, it has been argued, there has to be something in the story, some reason for it. Glastonbury has citizens who will tell you that they believe it literally. The reason why Joseph is said to have come to Britain is the simplest possible. He did come. Ray Burrows, a deeply rooted inhabitant, told me:

'One sign of being accepted here is that you get a nickname. And we don't say Joseph of Arimathea, we say Joe 'mathea. He's one of us.'

The foremost authority on the legend, Professor Valerie Lagorio, has allowed a 'very remote possibility' that these naive believers are right. They suggest that the wealthy Joseph made his money in the tin trade with Cornwall, and undertook voyages to Britain for that reason. Some add that he was related to Mary, and that on one of his voyages he brought the young Jesus with him. William Blake is commonly thought to refer to this latter notion in four famous lines:

> And did those feet in ancient time
> Walk upon England's mountains green?
> And was the holy Lamb of God
> On England's pleasant pastures seen?

The visit of Jesus seems to be quite a late idea. It may have arisen from an Abbey chronicle reporting a vision in which he was said to have dedicated the first church on the site. A spiritual presence was misunderstood by some latter-day reader as a literal one. Sceptics have alleged also that a schoolteacher in Priddy, on the Mendip hills, wrote a play for her pupils in which she imagined Jesus coming to their village, and the visit, like other fantasies, became an 'ancient Somerset legend'.

But to go back to Joseph, whose presence here actually is a legend (whatever germ of fact it may harbour) and a fairly ancient one. It appears piecemeal during the late twelfth and the early thirteenth centuries. Towards the year 1200 a Burgundian poet, Robert de Boron, wrote a narrative in French verse relating how Joseph acquired the Grail and how, after various adventures, it was started on its long journey to the Vales of 'Avaron' or Avalon, meaning central Somerset where Glastonbury was one day to be. Why that name *Avalon*? We shall see in a moment. Robert is drawing on a Glastonbury tradition, but he says nothing of Joseph coming to Britain himself. Some years later, another romancer does bring him to Britain, though not clearly to Glastonbury. Some years later again, an Abbey chronicler puts it in writing that he arrived in Glastonbury in AD 63. But that date and other particulars cannot be reconciled with the Grail stories. Amazing though it may sound, I don't think the plain statement that Joseph brought the Grail to Glastonbury is made by any author of note before Tennyson. When the tale took shape in such a fragmented, contradictory way, it is hard to explain what happened as a simple process of writer copying from writer with improvements. It is easier to think of a common source further back which different writers exploited differently. Even so, the question why Joseph should have been chosen as either Grail-bearer or missionary to Britain has never been convincingly answered.

Whatever the truth behind these riddles, the word *Avalon* stands out sharply. It was at the Abbey that the evocative name came firmly to earth. It was at the Abbey, also, that Glastonbury forged its most famous link with Arthur. The two events were closely related. As to the Arthurian link, some would give 'forged' a sense I do not imply myself.

The Abbey ruins are in a forty-acre rectangle enclosed by the High Street, Magdalene Street, and two residential roads. In its medieval glory it was a Benedictine house on a grand scale, the largest religious community in the land, or an equal-first with Westminster. The saying went that if its abbot could marry the Abbess of Shaftesbury they would have more land than the King of England. Glastonbury's great church, nearly 600 feet long, was surpassed only by St Paul's Cathedral in London. Not much is left of it today. In 1539 Henry VIII seized the Abbey, hanging its octogenarian abbot, and a couple of decades later it passed from the Crown into private hands. A series of owners who cared nothing for preservation used the buildings as a quarry for marketable stone.

Stanley Austin, the last private owner, lived in Abbey House at the eastern end of the site. In 1907 he put the whole property up for sale. The auctioneer's notice, with odd insensitivity, was devoted almost entirely to the house and merely added, at the foot, 'Interesting ruins in grounds.' Local lore tells of a Glastonbury miracle. A rich American lady wanted to buy the remnant of the Abbey—reputedly, to transplant it to America—but missed a rail connection and arrived at the sale too late. The property was acquired by a bidder who was pledged to hold it on behalf of the Church of England, and who transferred it to the Bath and Wells Diocesan Trust in 1908. Since then the Abbey has been well cared for, and today it has an abundant stream of visitors, more than 100,000 a year, and receives two annual pilgrimages, besides being used in the summer as an open-air theatre.

When all legend-weaving has been discounted, it remains more than likely that this place was the home of the first Christian community in England: the first, at any rate, that survived. Celtic British monks were here in the sixth century, perhaps the fifth, and hermits probably lived round about before there was any organized monastery. It is also likely that there is something in those stories about the Tor neighbourhood, and an even earlier Christian settlement existed in that part of the Isle. Some think the buildings found by Rahtz on the Tor's summit were monastic rather than secular. However, the main community was certainly on the Abbey site when the slowly-encroaching Saxons reached this area, in a year chronicled as 658. By then they had become Christians themselves, and they did not destroy the place, they took it over in a respectful spirit. As a result Glastonbury is the one religious

Opposite
Glastonbury Abbey. View of the ruins from inside the Lady Chapel, which
marks the site of the mysterious Old Church.

centre in England having Christian continuity since Late Roman times or nearly so. The Saxon-Celtic partnership at Glastonbury was a novel thing. To quote Armitage Robinson, a notable Somerset historian, the monastery became a temple of reconciliation between long-hostile peoples, the ancestors of the Welsh and Cornish, the ancestors of the English; and it drew in Irishmen as well. Here symbolically the United Kingdom was born. Here too, three centuries later, St Dunstan became abbot and launched the rebuilding of an England that had suffered at the hands of the Danes. The great medieval Abbey was rooted in his work.

But how does this connect with the legends? Where was it all supposed to have sprung from originally, and why?

In the Middle Ages, a religious house of such antiquity and importance might be expected to improve its history so as to claim a greater antiquity and a more distinctive importance. Glastonbury's monks did so. Sometimes drawing on real early tradition, sometimes not, they built up a copious list of holy men and women alleged to have visited the place, or lived there, or been buried there, quite apart from Joseph of Arimathea. Most of this mythology coalesced round a single fact. Throughout the monastery's existence, from Celtic times onward, a church had stood within the precinct which was so ancient that there was no authentic record of its foundation. It was on the ground now occupied by the shell of the Lady Chapel. Abbey documents tell truly or falsely of kings granting charters, and saints coming to pay their respects, but when they came, the church was always there already. Because of its long priority to the rest of the buildings, it was called the Old Church.

Basically it was a rustic structure of wattle-work—twigs bound with clay—but timber reinforcements and a casing of lead had transformed the fabric and preserved it. It was dedicated to the Virgin Mary, a significant detail, because her cultus was hardly known in England before Norman times. History shows that this dedication is more likely to have been a product of Late Roman influence than of any phase of Christian devotion during the next few centuries. That is, it fits in well with a very early date for the Old Church.

William of Malmesbury, a monastic librarian who made a stay at Glastonbury about 1129, wrote of the veneration in which the Old Church was held. His account tantalizingly describes its floor:

> One can observe all over the floor stones, artfully interlaced in the forms of triangles or squares and sealed with lead; I do no harm to religion if I believe some sacred mystery is contained beneath them.

William's cryptic phrases may hint at something to do with alchemy. They also supply the only real support—not much, though—for another modern theory, that the Abbey was laid out on a plan reflecting knowledge of a 'sacred geometry' employed also at Stonehenge and on other unexpected sites.

In 1184 a fire swept the Abbey and most of the buildings perished, including the Old Church. So we can never retrieve its floor pattern or establish its real age archaeologically. But speculation about it had long been active at the time of the fire, and did not cease with its destruction. Even before William of Malmesbury, a monastic writer had claimed that it was not built by human hands, but 'prepared by God himself'. William preferred to avoid sheer miracle. He was inclined to think it dated from the second century when papal emissaries, according to an ancient but dubious account, came to Britain at the request of a king named Lucius. If this royal Briton existed, he may have been a chief holding office under the Romans, but he probably did not. William also took note, if rather cautiously, of a belief that the foundation was earlier still, and that 'disciples of Christ' had built the Old Church in the first century.

This was how Joseph was brought in, though not at once. William left the disciples nameless. The belief which he mentioned, however, reappeared in Robert de Boron's tale of early Christians bringing the Grail to Avalon. They were presented as companions of Joseph, and it was in a new edition of William's book, compiled at the Abbey during the thirteenth century, that Joseph was brought to Glastonbury by name and credited with heading the 'disciples' who built the Old Church. The edition was much expanded and contained a great deal which William would not have approved, but he had supplied the opening that let Joseph into Abbey records and gave him his official status. This apostolic sanctity helped the permanent weaving of other saints into the Abbey's lavish pseudo-history.

When the Old Church vanished in the flames, the monks hastened to build the Lady Chapel to take its place, with the same Mary dedication. The site was called the holiest earth of England. Joseph himself was a cherished tradition only, his grave being unknown, but a crypt below the chapel was eventually made into another one for him. When you enter today, going down the steps, you are in Joseph's part of the structure, with a modern floor and altar. In the last decades of the Abbey's life, pilgrims used to descend to his shrine for private prayer. A guide printed in 1520 lists a number of miraculous cures, the most agreeably honest case being that of John Gyldon, partly paralyzed and unable to speak, who was cured after visiting Joseph's shrine . . . except that his left arm continued to hurt a little.

But why Avalon? and what else about Arthur?

'Avalon', formerly spelt with a double-*l*, is a word with Celtic roots meaning the 'apple' place. The French region of Burgundy has a town so called. The name was used as an equivalent for the Welsh 'Avallach', which stood for a mythical island and probably, though not certainly, has the same meaning, apples being magical fruit. *Insula Avallonis* in Latin, the Isle of Avalon, makes its first known appearance in a highly imaginative *History of the Kings of Britain* by Geoffrey of Monmouth. Writing towards 1138, and professing to cover eighteen centuries of the remote past, Geoffrey created (among much else)

King Arthur's official biography, the framework of the romances. In this he speaks of Arthur's sword being forged in Avalon, and, more importantly, says that after his last fatal battle the King was taken there for his wounds to be attended to. He never tells his readers what finally became of Arthur. In a poem composed later he adds more about the wonderful apple-island, saying that it was ruled by the enchantress Morgen—Morgan le Fay, as she becomes in the Arthurian tales—and that she took the wounded King into her care. The poem still makes no commitment as to his fate, and is vague as to the isle's whereabouts, though it seems to lie somewhere over western waters.

When Geoffrey's inventive *History* became popular, it established Avalon as Arthur's last destination. Caradoc, the author who told of Melwas kidnapping Guinevere, had already connected Arthur with Glastonbury. Moreover he had referred to the place as an island or near-island in Arthur's time, and given it a sort of Otherworld quality . . . or recognized an Otherworld quality that was older. The conclusion that Glastonbury *was* Avalon was an easy and natural one to draw. It may have been drawn long before, the more readily as this is apple-growing country, but evidence fails us. At any rate, in 1190 or early '91 the monks of the Abbey clinched the matter by announcing that they had found Arthur's bones. Glastonbury had indeed been his last destination. It *was* the true Avalon.

ARTHUR'S GRAVE

The background of the monks' announcement is most imperfectly known. Hitherto, so far as any record goes, the location of the King's burial had been shrouded in mystery. That is the testimony of a Welsh poem, and of William of Malmesbury, who, besides writing much on the Old Church, wrote a little on Arthur. According to a folk-belief Arthur had no grave, because he hadn't died at all. If he was not in the enchanted island he was asleep in a cave, and he would return to lead his people again—meaning, by now, the Welsh, Cornish and Bretons, descendants of the Celtic Britons of old.

But, the Abbey averred, the grave's whereabouts had always been known to some. Not at Glastonbury itself, doubtless because the dominant Anglo-Saxons had effaced all memory of a man who was no hero of theirs, but . . . to some, on the Celtic fringes. A Welsh or Breton bard finally divulged the secret to King Henry II. Arthur was buried in the graveyard of Glastonbury Abbey south of the Lady Chapel, at a great depth, between two monumental pillars. Henry passed this news to the Abbot, and a few years later, prompted by hints from other sources, the monks excavated the spot. They dug down seven feet and unearthed a stone slab. Under it was a lead cross about a foot long*, with a Latin inscription: HIC IACET SEPULTUS INCLITUS REX ARTURIUS IN INSULA AVALONIA, 'Here lies buried the renowned King Arthur in the Isle of Avalon.' Nine feet farther down they found a rough coffin made from a hollowed-out log. Inside were the bones of a tall man who had seemingly been killed by a blow on the head, because the skull was damaged. Some smaller bones, and a scrap of hair that crumbled away when touched, were explained as Guinevere's. The bones were placed in caskets, and in 1278 they were transferred, during a state visit by Edward I, to a black marble tomb before the high altar of the main Abbey church. There they remained till the rifling and vandalizing after the dissolution. Today a notice-board marks the spot, and occasionally people lay flowers there.

Most historians, though not all, have dismissed this affair as a fraud and a publicity stunt. It happened soon after the fire, when money was needed for rebuilding. King Arthur's grave would attract visitors and donations, so King Arthur's grave was duly concocted. Another motive was perhaps to discourage the Welsh in their resistance to the kings of England, since if Arthur was demonstrably dead, he would not be coming back to aid them.

While both theories are plausible, that is all they are: theories. There is no evidence that the monks did exploit the grave to raise funds, or that it was ever

*The size of the cross is noted by John Leland, who saw it in the sixteenth century.

Opposite
Glastonbury Abbey. South side of the Lady Chapel. Two present-day paths, at
right angles, traverse the ground of the monastic cemetery. The grave claimed
as Arthur's was discovered near the point where they intersect.

Above left
Camden's drawing of the lead cross found in Arthur's grave. Often dismissed
as a twelfth-century forgery. However, the style and irregularity of the
lettering, and the Latin form of the name 'Arthur', could suggest an earlier date.

Above right
Glastonbury Abbey. The place in the middle of the great church where a tomb
was made for the reputed bones of Arthur and Guinevere.

used to dishearten the Welsh. In 1958 the archaeologist Ralegh Radford
showed that the account of the excavation, if somewhat heightened, was
basically in keeping with the known history of the graveyard. In 1962–3 he
excavated the site himself, and found traces of the monks' digging so long
before. Deep down, at a spot suggesting a person of importance, he discovered stone slabs such as were used to line ancient burials, and these were
disarranged, as if a large object—the coffin?—had been dragged out.
Radford's trench has long been refilled, of course. The grave is under a level
lawn, fifty feet or so from the south door of the Lady Chapel, near the inter-
section of two paths.

This modern exploration destroyed the charge of a complete fraud by the
monks, though I am bound to remark that you can find scholars' books,
written years afterwards, which still refuse to admit it and ignore Radford's
work, or consign it to references which the reader probably won't look up.

Yes, there was a grave, and it could have been as early as the fifth or sixth century when, reputedly, Arthur lived. But whose was it in fact? The identification depends on the inscribed cross. It has vanished, but we have a drawing of one side of it in a book by William Camden published in 1607. A description written soon after the exhumation says it mentioned Guinevere, whereas her name is not in Camden's drawing, but it may have been on the other side. The lettering is untidy and rather crude, and might well suggest a date long before 1190. Moreover the Latin version of 'Arthur', Arturius, was not the normal one at that time, and has only been found in a document of the seventh century. Under medieval conditions it would have taken an astonishing forger to hit on an archaism like this and put it in the inscription.

At present we can get no further. One possibility remains, that the cross itself might be rediscovered. It did not vanish among the loot of the dissolution. Camden saw it and drew it, and two hundred years ago it was in the possession of a Mr Hughes, one of the cathedral clergy in Wells. Does it still lie in some lumber-room, unrecognized?

An End, A Beginning

The curious thing about Glastonbury—one of the curious things, anyhow—is that all its legends and fancies can be refuted, yet always something is left over, a trailing loose end that trips the critic.

Thus, the monks alleged a first-century Christian advent. No real evidence exists, and Joseph can easily be set aside as a medieval figment, if you are so inclined. Yet we can say positively, now, that the lake-villages were there at about the right time, that the area had sea connections and foreign trade, that a voyager might well have come here. Not being archaeologists, the monks had no apparent way to know this. If they merely happened to make such a good guess, it was a rare and truly remarkable happening. Conversely, if they actually had records going back so far, the sceptic who accuses them of making it all up is in obvious trouble.

The Chalice Well mythos is largely fantasy. Even the word 'Chalice', in this context, is a fairly recent invention. Yet the water does have a reddish tinge, and is unlike other water in Glastonbury, flowing from a different source.

Caradoc's story of the kidnap of Guinevere by a ruler of Somerset looks like a pure fairy-tale. Yet we know, now, that something which may have been a fort stood on the Tor at about the right time, and this knowledge depends on archaeology, uncovering buried foundations which Caradoc (on the face of it) could not have seen.

The Thorn legend is late, and the Thorn can be explained as a freak. Yet it really does blossom at Christmas, more or less; it really is unique among English trees; and if we look for an ancestry, the only trees it resembles are in Joseph's country, or near it.

Or turn to modern ideas. Archaeologists have poured scorn on the Tor maze, usually, it must be confessed, without looking. But once again, its complex pattern can be constructed on the Tor, 'quite convincingly', in Professor Rahtz's judgment. One of its most intemperate critics has admitted as much, and the admission is fatal. There can hardly be many other hills where the same can be done (indeed, are there any?) and the fact that it *can* be done at Glastonbury, of all places, is beyond shrugging off.

Even the wilder modern fancies, so vulnerable in a general way, don't collapse entirely. I doubt if Nostradamus actually does refer to the Zodiac, but he has lines which can be construed as doing so. And however far-fetched sacred geometry may be, William of Malmesbury does hint at a secret enciphered in the floor design of the Old Church. It would be hard to find many medieval churches of which the same was said in a contemporary text.

In each individual case the facts that resist the rational onslaught might be accidental. If, however, you take them together, King Arthur's Avalon does seem accident-prone. Glastonbury has been called holy, historic, fraudulent, and other things. I would add 'impish'. That still holds for Arthur's grave. It is manifestly suspect. It can be dismissed, and it often has been dismissed, as a fake. Yet the monks did discover an early grave, and 'Arturius' on the cross is a genuine archaism which a forger in those days would have been unlikely to get hold of, or recognize or use if he did.

One further point has always impressed me. The theory of a fake depends on the assumption that Arthur's grave had prestige value. Otherwise, why go to such trouble? No doubt it did have prestige value. But if grounds for doubt or suspicion existed, why did no one dispute it, denying Glastonbury a false glory and perhaps claiming the glory elsewhere? Why did the Welsh, in particular, let English monks get away with a monstrous lie about a hero whom the Welsh claimed as theirs? Other Glastonbury claims, to the bones of St Dunstan for instance, were disputed and disputed effectively. Whatever the truth about Arthur's grave, it seems clear to me that there was a prior tradition, lingering probably among a few bards, which could not be challenged once it leaked out to Henry II. The contrast with other Arthurian 'sites' is marked. Some of them are all too multiple. We hear of rival Camelots, rival scenes of Arthur's last battle, and so forth. But all the centuries of Arthurian legend-making produced, for practical purposes, only the one grave.

This leads to an odd reversal. However much Glastonbury is discounted, Arthurian themes are here most apparent, most visibly drawn together: the King and the Grail, the Queen and Lancelot. Nevertheless, by beginning at Glastonbury we begin at the end, at the King's departure. To explore both his legendary career and whatever facts may underlie it, we must go elsewhere. Even here Glastonbury can point the way, as we shall see.

Meanwhile, though, we have a loose end of our own. What about that prophecy of rebirth, said to have been uttered on a death-bed in the neighbourhood by an untraceable monk, Austin Ringwode, in 1587? I don't know, but I have a notion. A year or two before that, a Jesuit, William Weston, visited these parts and a passage in his memoirs deserves quotation.

> I sought hospitality once at the house of a certain Catholic. He was a very old man, his hair completely white. He was at least an octogenarian. Before Henry VIII destroyed and did away with the monasteries, he had been in the employment of the abbey of Glastonbury, either as a servant or as the holder of an administrative office in some department.... In addition to other things which the old man was able to seize and save, as it were, from the conflagration was a certain cross, venerable and hallowed not so much for its material interest—though it was worked with gold and valuable gems—as because it encased the remains of revered saints. Its principal relic was one of the nails with which our Saviour Christ was fastened to the Cross, and an almost immemorial tradition held that it had been brought to England by St Joseph of Arimathea and his companions . . .
>
> The old man's house was three or four miles from the ancient monastery, but barely a mile from the place which, according to tradition, St Joseph of Arimathea and his companions had chosen for their dwelling. This was on a high hill, and its old foundations and broken fragments of masonry can be seen there today. He told me how occasionally he would visit it out of piety and devotion, climbing up, not on his feet, but on his knees; and how he would take with him the cross and the reliquary containing the nail—'my protection,' he called it, 'against the molestation of spirits.' Indeed, it was possible to hear there the groanings, sighs and wailing voices of people in distress, so that he thought it must be a kind of approach or vestibule for souls passing into the pains of Purgatory. As a constant religious ceremony he kept a lamp suspended and always burning in a part of the house which looked towards the hill. All these stories and many others the old man told me, so that I stayed with him two days or more, entertained and enchanted by his conversation far more than I had expected.

Weston, writing from memory after arduous journeying, is confused about distances, but several points emerge. It is clear that the folk-tradition of Joseph which the old man reported ignored the claim of the Abbey chroniclers, by locating the original settlement somewhere else. The uncanny 'high hill' can hardly be anything but the Tor, since its entrance to a purgatorial Underworld is a palpable Christian echo of the legend of Gwyn, whom St Collen tried to exorcize. The 'broken fragments of masonry' might have been anywhere from the lower slope to the summit, but if the old man climbed to them on his knees they were surely not far up, not far above what is now Well

House Lane in the valley between the Tor and Chalice Hill. We are glimpsing that tradition of early Christian settlement which is also glimpsed in Arthurian romance, when Lancelot meets hermits close to the spring, and later becomes a hermit himself, in what seems to be the same little valley.

A fourteenth-century list of the Abbey's treasures includes several unlikely relics of Christ, but no nail. By the end of its life the accumulation of such things had evidently gone further. But who can blame this old man, who would not accept the Reformation, for wanting to keep mementoes? He can hardly have survived much longer after Weston's visit. As an Abbey employee he had been part of the religious community, and local recollection could quickly have blurred distinctions and made him out to have been a monk. Was this Austin Ringwode? Was it he who ended his days, in 1587, prophesying that the Abbey would rise again?

2. Search for Camelot

THE HILL

SCALING GLASTONBURY TOR is easier now than it used to be. The National Trust has provided steps in the steeper and muddier bits. If you climb to the top, and stroll around the flat space where St Michael's tower stands, you survey a low-lying panorama of central Somerset—the Grail writer's Vales of Avalon—with an assortment of hills in the distance. To the north are the Mendips, famous for the Cheddar Caves and Gorge, and for Wookey Hole, where a Glastonbury monk turned the resident witch into a stalagmite. North-west is the solitary dome of Brent Knoll; more of that hereafter. Past Brent Knoll to the left, on a clear day, you can see across to the coast of Wales. South-west are the Polden Hills and the Quantocks and the approaches of Exmoor; more of that too hereafter. South-east, on the side away from the sea, is a line of hills on the fringes of Dorset, and in front of them is another. Camelot.

From the Tor it is difficult to pick Camelot out, unless you know fairly precisely where to look and what to look for. Though isolated, it blends into the hills behind. The best way to identify it is to face a reservoir at the Tor's foot and run an imaginary line out from the right-hand side of it to the horizon. Then, given a reasonably clear day, you can distinguish a dark patch of wood and an open hilltop rising slightly above.

Camelot—and that name for it is time-honoured, whatever its aptitude or implication—is the hill-fort Cadbury Castle, above the village of South Cadbury. Let me make one thing clear at the outset, there was never a castle here in the medieval sense. The word is employed as it is in quite a number of places in south and south-west England, to mean a hill defended by earthwork ramparts and ditches. The hill itself is the castle. This one was settled and fortified by British Celts during the last centuries BC. You get to it by leaving the A303

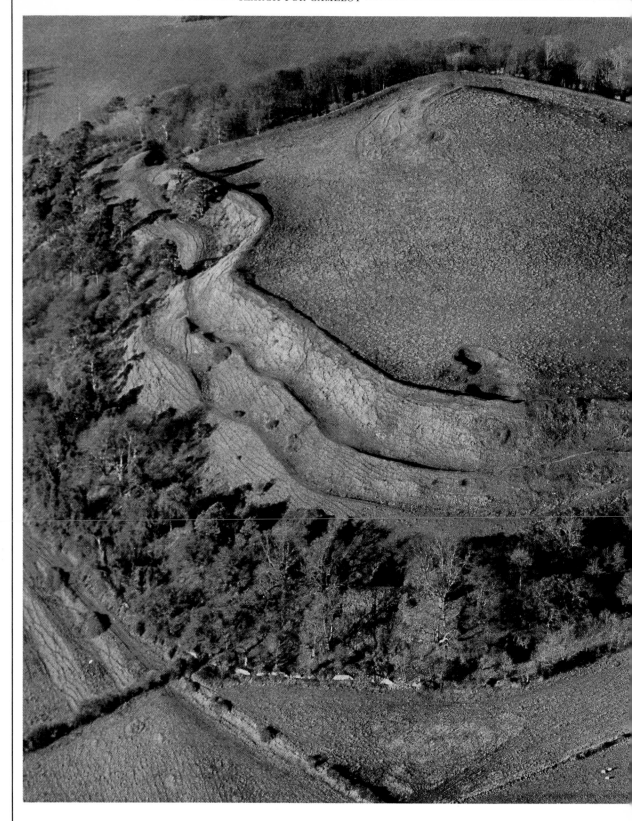

Cadbury-Camelot. The Somerset hill-fort Cadbury Castle, stated by Leland in 1542 to have been Arthur's headquarters, a belief examined archaeologically in 1966–70. The ramparts are now largely overgrown with woods, but, besides the three partially in the open, a fourth can be seen by looking down from above.

between Sparkford and Wincanton, on a road running south through the village, past the church (one of its curates, in the eighteenth century, walked out and joined the Hell-Fire Club), to the place where a path goes up the hill. There is only one such place. The path climbs through trees, becoming, after heavy rain, exceedingly muddy, and emerges above on to eighteen acres of open grass. The woods are best in springtime when they are full of bluebells and primroses. On this side they have almost blotted out the ancient pattern of earthworks, but you can still see the four huge ramparts out in the open by circling round to the left from the top of the path.

The enclosure within the ramparts goes on rising to a plateau, about on a level with the summit of Glastonbury Tor. Like the Tor it overlooks an expanse, which includes the Fleet Air Arm base at Yeovilton, so that Navy helicopters and jets are apt to pass noisily overhead. Towards the Bristol Channel the Tor itself stands plain in the distance, with its tower on top, and in clear conditions you can see past it to Brent Knoll. These hills are not far from lying along a straight line, and across the sea, roughly on the same line pro-longed, is the Welsh hill-fort of Dinas Powys. It has been suggested that all four hills, anciently inhabited, might have formed a chain of communication by beacon. One link at least has been tested. On a night in 1967 a fire lit on the heights of Cadbury was seen without much trouble from the top of the Tor, and when there were fewer lights in the landscape, such signalling would have been no trouble at all.

In 1542 the Tudor traveller John Leland, describing his itinerary through England, wrote: 'At the very south end of the church of South-Cadbyri stan-deth Camallate, sometime a famous town or castle.... The people can tell nothing there but that they have heard say Arthur much resorted to Camalat.' Some have thought this a mere guess prompted by the village-name 'Camel' which occurs a few miles away. But Leland's spelling with an *a* in the last syllable may echo a local pronunciation that can still be heard, with the *a* sounded as in 'father', and the hill definitely has an Arthurian aura, whatever the real age of its folklore.

It claims, for instance, the oldest known version of the cave-legend, the popular rather than literary version of Arthur's immortality. He lies asleep in a cavern closed with iron gates, or maybe golden ones, and if you pass it on the right night of the year they stand open, and you can see him inside. There may

Opposite above
Glastonbury Tor from the air, showing some of the paths or terraces that run all the way round. One theory accounts for them by geological causes, another by medieval agriculture. A third view is that they are remnants of a vast earthwork maze, constructed for ritual purposes three or four thousand years ago.

Opposite below
Glastonbury Abbey. Ruins of the central arch of the great church, built in the thirteenth century. Chalice Hill is in the background.

Glastonbury Tor with the
setting sun behind it.

actually be a silted-up cave in the scarp on the south of the plateau. When a party of Victorian archaeologists visited Cadbury, an old man from the village asked them if they planned to take the King away.

On the left of the ascent path is Arthur's Well, and the highest part of the plateau has been Arthur's Palace since at least 1586. According to legend the ghosts of Arthur and his knights make a periodic nocturnal ride over the hilltop and down to Sutton Montis below, where the horses drink at a spring. This is reputed to happen on Midsummer Eve, or Midsummer Night, or Christmas Eve, or only every seventh year, so the ghosts may be difficult to catch riding. I have kept the vigil twice without seeing them, but perhaps I chose the wrong night; and I do recall walking along the uppermost rampart in pitch darkness, and hearing, far below in the woods, the sound of a flute.

Beneath the hill are remnants of an old track running towards Glastonbury. This is Arthur's Lane, or Hunting Causeway, and on rough winter nights, they say, a noise of spectral hooves and hounds can be heard along it. A small river, the Cam, flows between Cadbury and Sparkford, and has been proposed as the river 'Camlann', the Crooked Bank, scene of Arthur's last battle. Many years ago a farmer reported digging up skeletons huddled together in a field on that side of the hill.

REVELATIONS

Is this Camelot in any deeper or more serious sense? To begin with, in what sense could it be?

The actual name turns up first in medieval romances. No one knows where it came from. It might have been suggested by the Roman *Camulodunum*, though that meant Colchester in Essex, which even legend never reckons as Arthurian ground. Geoffrey of Monmouth, in his *History of the Kings of Britain*, gives a flamboyant description of Arthur's court at Caerleon in Wales, and the literary creators of Camelot doubtless took hints from this. As they present the place, it is a medieval dream-city which it would be futile to look for anywhere. Their own indications are conflicting. Guesses at Camelford in Cornwall and other towns are not so much mistaken as pointless. Winchester has often been favoured because it is Malory's Camelot, but Winchester fails for a reason that is more important in the appraisal of Cadbury. The Camelot of legend has a distinctive quality which is easy to overlook. It is

Opposite above
Glastonbury Abbey. Ruins towards the eastern end of the great church. The notice-board in the centre marks the site of the marble tomb where the reputed bones of Arthur and Guinevere were laid, during a visit by Edward I in 1278.

Opposite below
Brent Knoll, Somerset. An Iron Age hill-fort near the coast. In Arthurian legend this hill is called the Mount of Frogs, and is the home of three evil giants, slain by Sir Ider.

not England's capital city as, for a time, Winchester was; it is Arthur's personal residence. No one reigned there before him, apparently no one reigns there after him. Some say, indeed, that when he was gone the evil King Mark of Cornwall marched on Camelot and destroyed it.

An original Camelot, a far-off reality behind the legend, is conceivable on that basis. Not a city, or an established seat of government for successive rulers, but a place which an original Arthur made his headquarters. It was this possibility that gave Arthurian relevance to the excavations carried out in 1966–70. Among several investigators who had probed Cadbury before, the best known, though not in that role, was John Steinbeck. His lifelong interest in the Arthurian Legend appeared in some of his novels, and, towards the close of his life, in a retelling of parts of it. During visits to the West Country, he devised what he called his badger method of archaeology. On Cadbury and other hills he sought out the setts of badgers, and he would come with a shovel while the badger was inside, and fill up the entrance, whereupon the badger dug madly in all directions and threw up heaps of earth. Steinbeck would sift them and extract Roman coins and other objects. Or so he told me in a letter. Alas, he died before I met him, and I don't know whether he was having me on.

In the mid-1950s, without benefit of badgers, a local archaeologist named Mary Harfield put Cadbury in what was then a fresh light. Part of the summit enclosure had been ploughed up for crops. The topsoil was shallow and harboured a jumble of odds and ends of various ages. Mrs Harfield used to walk her dog over the hill. The dog's name was Caesar. While Caesar trotted about, she poked among the furrows with the ferrule of her umbrella, and collected a medley of flints and pottery shards. These were examined by Ralegh Radford, who was then giving attention to Glastonbury Abbey. More significant for Cadbury, as it turned out, was an excavation he had performed twenty years earlier at Tintagel, Arthur's legendary birthplace. On that Cornish headland he had found pottery of a type which he recognized again among Mrs Harfield's fragments. It was non-British ware of high quality, used for expensive goods such as wine and oil, and imported from the east Mediterranean. Further, it could be dated to the later part of the fifth century or the sixth. Its presence implied occupation by a household of wealth and standing, very likely a princely or royal one, at more or less the reputed time of Arthur.

Nothing came of this for years. In 1965, however, the Camelot Research Committee was formed. Sir Mortimer Wheeler was president, Dr Radford was chairman, I was secretary. In five summer seasons of work beginning in 1966, excavations were carried out under the direction of Leslie Alcock, now Professor Alcock. They were financed from a variety of sources—learned societies, the Pilgrim Trust, facilities fees from the media, contributions from the public at large. One point is still worth making. Alcock came in for criticism (too mild a word, really) from other archaeologists who complained, among much else, that as far as the public was concerned Camelot meant only the Camelot of romance, and when people realized it wasn't there they would feel cheated and lose interest, and it would be harder to raise funds for archaeology generally. The critics were wrong about that as they were wrong about everything. The level of public donations rose each year, while the flood of visitors was so massive and unrelenting that we had to put up a marquee for them and provide full-time guides. I recall being telephoned by someone speaking for Warner Brothers, who explained that they wanted to make a map for the film version of the musical *Camelot*, and asked where Camelot was. I replied 'Somerset', and, in the film, the map is briefly displayed with Camelot in Somerset—my sole contribution to Hollywood.

As expected, most of what came to light belonged to the pre-Roman Iron Age, when centuries of occupation on the plateau imprinted the bedrock with post-holes, foundation trenches and refuse pits, and scattered artefacts among them. The same period built up several strata of fortification. A macabre and intriguing find, near the south-east bend of the top rampart, was a human sacrifice, a young male skeleton rammed head-downwards into a pit with further rampart-building on top. The purpose of such a sacrifice would have been supernatural support for the wall. In Geoffrey's *History*, Merlin makes his youthful début as an intended sacrifice with that very object, and the story may suggest a real tradition of the pagan custom witnessed by the Cadbury skeleton.

A more puzzling discovery was that Cadbury carried on unchanged and untouched during the Roman occupation of southern Britain which began under the emperor Claudius in AD 43. The Romans eventually stormed and captured it, but not till about two decades later. It figured in some last gesture of resistance, perhaps an offshoot of the revolt of Queen Boudicca in 60–61. We might picture a British chief holding out in the hills and marshes like Hereward the Wake, with Cadbury as a stronghold of his tiny realm. In those days, one Briton is on record as a nuisance to Rome who cannot be associated with the known opposition. His name was Arviragus. The poet Juvenal mentions him. Medieval authors, led by Geoffrey of Monmouth, inflated him into a major monarch contemporary with Claudius and his successor Nero. He was not that, but was he the lord of an independent enclave in Somerset? According to Glastonbury Abbey, Joseph of Arimathea was granted his plot of ground in the year 63 by a king in those parts who was independent of Rome. Before the Cadbury discovery, such a king at such a date seemed out of the question. Now, however, he is just possible, and Abbey chroniclers give his name as . . . Arviragus.

No, it isn't history. It's simply one more of those Avalonian oddities that stand in the way of the would-be annihilator.

To revert to more solid matters, when the Romans did storm the hill, they deported its inhabitants and resettled them near the foot, doubtless to prevent its being used as a base in any further rebellion. For about four hundred years Cadbury was vacant or nearly so. It had no function. But in the troubles of the post-Roman era, when Britons were compelled to look to their own safety, Cadbury had plain attractions in its defensive strength and its command of a wide area. If, also, it had once been a sort of British Masada, the scene of a last heroic struggle, it would have been a natural choice for a leader trying to reassert British power.

From whatever motive or motives, such a leader did choose it. Little by little, excavation confirmed the pottery-attested establishment, the potential Camelot. It showed that in the 460s or somewhat later, but probably not much after 500, a timber hall was built on the plateau in the 'Arthur's Palace' area. A gate-house was built at the old entrance, not where you enter the enclosure today, but on the south-west where a gap in the top rampart marks the spot. To cast an eye from gate to hall is to appreciate how some of the Arthurian stories fit better in what *may* be their authentic context than they do in the literary setting of later times. In the Welsh tale *Culhwch and Olwen* ('Culhwch' is pronounced 'Kil-hooch', with the *ch* as in 'loch'), the hero comes to the gateway of Arthur's court and demands admission. The gate-keeper tells him that everybody is sitting down to eat in the hall and he won't go to ask Arthur whether Culhwch can be let in. At Cadbury it makes good sense. The hall was hundreds of yards from the gate, up a steep slope. The gate-keeper might well have demurred at such a long walk, especially if it was raining.

More important than the hall or the gate-house was a larger discovery. During the same period a new system of defences was superimposed on the top bank. Today everything has long been put back and it lies embedded again, but in the course of the excavations it was exposed to view by a series of cuts at different places. It was a wall sixteen feet thick going round the entire perimeter, nearly three-quarters of a mile. Its courses of unmortared stone incorporated pieces of Roman masonry, and it was bound by a framework of wooden beams. There were probably breastworks and platforms, possibly watchtowers, though the wood has long since rotted away. This rampart was no crude heaping-up of earth, it was a fairly sophisticated structure, Celtic rather than Roman in style. The careful arrangement of the stones, and the felling of trees and shaping of beams, would have called for a vast amount of labour.

At first Alcock interpreted the site in this period as an army base. He was thinking mainly of evidence for British resistance to the barbarian Saxons which stopped their advance at 'Mount Badon' somewhere about the year 500, Badon being arguably in the Bath area. The favoured theory about Arthur, based on Welsh tradition, was that he was a commander-in-chief rather than a king, and that he led the resistance and won the victory. Hence he could be accepted on logical and strategic grounds as the master of the unique Cadbury fortress.

Critics retorted that its uniqueness was an assumption due purely to insufficient data. They insinuated that when more hill-forts were excavated, it would turn out that others had been refortified similarly in the same period and Cadbury was not special. That, however, kept failing to happen. Over the next few years a number were indeed excavated. Some had been reoccupied in the fifth century or the sixth, sometimes there had been a refurbishing of the old defences, usually on a small scale. But there was not a single instance in England or Wales of a stone-and-timber system of the same type. A few British and Pictish ones came to light in Scotland, but all were smaller, the British ones substantially so. Also, none had a gate-house. As far as anyone knows Cadbury is unparalleled in its size and structure, completely so in the former territory of Roman Britain, though it must be owned that there are diehards who continue to evade the fact.

Lecturing at the British Academy in 1982, Alcock offered a tentative revised assessment. On the one hand he now deprecated talk of Arthur personally. On the other he suggested, in the light of work on northern sites, that Cadbury-Camelot might be better explained politically, as the headquarters of a king with resources of manpower unequalled, so far as present knowledge goes, in the Britain of his time.

It has emerged fairly clearly that when Leland spoke of Cadbury as Camelot, in 1542, he was not merely guessing. Somehow he hit on what is easily the most suitable hill throughout Britain, the only credible Camelot in the only credible sense. Even a modern archaeologist could never have detected the refortification merely by looking, without digging. Leland heard a real tradition reaching back through the centuries. It does not follow, though, that it originally included the magic names. By Leland's time the Arthurian Legend was so well known that a story of a great king living on the hill might have led him, or anyone, to jump to a conclusion about King Arthur and Camelot. How the nearby 'Camel' place-names fit in, or whether they do, I don't feel equal to discussing.

But perhaps we can say something about the kind of king the story would have indicated. Alcock noted one clue, fascinating though frail, in a Latin work called the *Historia Brittonum*, History of the Britons, compiled in North Wales early in the ninth century. This is often referred to as 'Nennius' because a monk of that name was credited with compiling it. Amid a mass of unconvincing traditions and outright legends, one royal figure comes dimly into view in the decades before Arthur, the British king Vortigern who gets the blame for letting the Saxons—the future English—into Britain. Despite much fantasy he seems to have been a real person. 'Vortigern' means 'over-chief' or 'over-king', and looks like a title or designation for a 'high king' in more or less the Irish sense, paramount at least in name over a number of regional rulers.

Now Vortigern, we are told, tried to build himself a fortress in the mountains of Snowdonia. The passage states that the royal workmen assembled 'timber and stones', evidently thought of as the proper materials for a fifth-century high king's stronghold. Timber and stones are the distinctive materials at Cadbury. It may have been the fortification of another high king, a successor of Vortigern. A British ruler later than 460 is unlikely to have wielded power over much more than a region: over, say, what was once the kingdom of Dumnonia and is now the West Country, the most that can be seriously proposed as the domain of the lord of Cadbury. He might still, however, have claimed a vague suzerainty over other rulers in other parts of ex-Roman Britain. There is no proof as to when precisely it broke up into quite separate kingdoms.

Who actually was this king who refortified Cadbury? Are we face to face with Arthur or not?

3. Shapes in the Mist

WE ARE NOW MOVING into a baffling half-light. It is vital to be sure what we are talking about and what questions to ask. In the Cadbury-Camelot refortification we at least have something large, solid and exceptional. It is *there*, and it didn't grow by itself, and it wasn't created by story-tellers. A British leader of stature existed to put it there, to organize the manpower and the material resources. We can properly look for a candidate to fill that role. But can we admit Arthur as such?

After all, he is normally conceived as a legend, and rightly. Geoffrey of Monmouth, towards 1138, concocted his pseudo-biography in the *History of the Kings of Britain*, and medieval writers all over western Europe spun their romances more or less fitting him into it. The direct question 'Did King Arthur exist?' cannot really be given a direct answer. 'Yes' implies that the monarch of romance existed, and he didn't. 'No' implies that he is simply a medieval fiction, and that too is unwarranted. The difficulty lies in the medieval writers' attitude to old stories. A modern historical novelist aims at authenticity, the romancers did not. Whatever the actual period of the story, they updated it, dressing it up in the costume of their own time, introducing castles and heraldry and tournaments and chivalry and literary love-conventions. King Arthur's impossibility in his medieval guise doesn't disprove an original, if a very different one, in the fifth or sixth century. To make progress with the problem we need to stand back a little, to ask not 'Did King Arthur exist?' but 'How did his Legend originate, what facts is it rooted in?' Inquiry along that line can shed light both on Arthur and on Cadbury.

The Britons, who belonged to the Roman Empire for over three hundred years, were separated from it in practice about 410, though more years were to

An expanse of country in southern Scotland, much of it formerly covered by the Caledonian Wood or Forest of Celidon, one of the places where a battle allegedly fought by Arthur can be located with fair confidence.

pass before the breach was accepted as final. For a while they managed their own government without disaster. This is where Vortigern finds his place. The high king may have begun as a chieftain or official and exploited connections made under the Empire. Like other parts of the Roman West, Britain was harassed by barbarian raiders, mainly Picts from what is now Scotland, and Saxons from the coastlands across the North Sea. Following Roman precedents, the Britons employed one set of barbarians to hold off others. From the 420s onward increasing numbers of Saxons (that word also covers related Angles and Jutes, together with minor groupings, all collectively ancestors of the English) were settled in the east and south-east as auxiliaries or *foederati*, treaty troops. Many more arrived without authorization and their hosts could not or would not maintain them all. Towards the middle of the fifth century they got out of hand, and Britain slid into a phase of confusion, with Saxons and allied Picts, no longer held off, raiding across the country at will.

Somewhere about 460, they apparently stopped raiding and withdrew for a while into their authorized settlements. The Britons revived. A certain Ambrosius Aurelianus—a Roman name, hinting at a leadership with imperial sympathies—led a counter-attack against the Saxon enclaves. Decades of obscure fluctuations ensued. In parts of the former Roman land the Saxons were consolidating, and they were gaining fresh footholds along the south coast. Much of the process was very likely peaceable if not amicable. But here and there, the Britons' counter-action kept a sporadic warfare in being, and around the end of the fifth century the aforesaid British success at a hill called Badon was followed by a phase of relative equilibrium.

Hazy as all this is, we can see that the Arthurian Legend, which is unique in Europe, is grounded on a unique train of events. Alone among Rome's provincial peoples, the Britons became self-governing before the barbarians moved in, recovered and fought back when they did, and were partially successful. In the latter part of the fifth century, most of the country was still theirs, allowing space at least for an Arthur to flourish. Success, moreover, implies leadership and effective power, which could not have been confined to the one man we can confidently name, Ambrosius. And Ambrosius was not a king himself. Legend long afterwards made him so, but with no basis. Alcock suggested that he was a commander employed by some predominant ruler, perhaps a high king holding office after Vortigern. One question of course is obvious: If, when Ambrosius was active, he was not a king himself, who was? But setting that aside, Arthur as a British leader during this period, a patriotic champion, does belong intelligibly in a real context. So does the royal refortifier of Cadbury with his mighty stronghold. The latter existed, the former may have. To decide whether they are, or might be, or could be the same person, we have to try to get closer to them.

HISTORIC DOUBTS

The natural first step is to try getting closer to Arthur, by considering Geoffrey's pseudo-biography and asking where he got his ideas from, if anywhere. He has Arthur conceived at Tintagel through Merlin's magic, some years after the death of Vortigern. Becoming king of Britain at the age of fifteen, Arthur subdues the Saxons and other marauders, conquers various countries, founds an order of knighthood, reigns with magnificence, is betrayed while fighting Romans in Gaul (France) by his deputy-ruler Mordred, crushes the traitor but is grievously wounded himself, and departs to Avalon. As to the time when all this is supposed to have happened, most of Geoffrey's clues converge on a period vaguely between 440 and 480. He gives 542 for Arthur's passing, but this is hopelessly inconsistent with the rest, and there is good reason to think it a mistake. 'Exact' dates in medieval texts are extremely liable to be garbled, and a French adapter of Geoffrey, who turns this one into the even more absurd 642, shows how flimsy it is. Pretty well everything else in Geoffrey's story makes his Arthur a fifth-century ruler.

If we compare this part of Geoffrey's book with the rest, we can see that he is probably drawing on older histories or what he likes to believe are histories. Except in some fabulous early chapters, he is always normally doing this, not just inventing out of nothing. But we can also see that he does it with flagrant irresponsibility and lavish exaggeration. He is not writing history himself and he can never be relied on for facts. The thing to do when contemplating his Arthur is not to imagine that anything he says is a true record, but to ask what history or supposed history he is using to create his fiction.

He knows something of the fifth-century British setting, however wildly he romanticizes and dramatizes it, but with Arthur himself his sources of inspiration are not always easy to be sure about. Traditions handed down by the Welsh supplied him with materials for bits of the story. The ninth-century *Historia Brittonum*, by Nennius or whoever, has a chapter speaking of Arthur as war-leader among the Britons' regional rulers and listing twelve battles won by him. Most of the place-names are obscure, but the first battles are probably in Lincolnshire, where a campaign against encroaching Angles would be quite credible. Another is in the 'Caledonian Wood' in southern Scotland, where Arthur could have been fighting Pictish allies of the Angles, and another is in Chester, where he could have been combating known Saxon raiding across the country. The list culminates in Badon, credited to his leadership. It is probably based on a Welsh poem extolling his deeds, real or imaginary, and since Badon was almost certainly in the south, it implies a tradition of widespread activity if not widespread rule. His status is not really defined. A later chronicle in Latin called the *Annales Cambriae*, or Annals of Wales, makes him the Badon victor again and adds the 'strife of Camlann' in which he fell.

Geoffrey has used both these texts, or something like them. However, they account for only about one-fifth of his Arthur story. He gives far more space to Arthur's warfare in Gaul, which is much more important, and nothing from Wales underlies this. While there is also Welsh poetry and saga matter—verses mentioning Arthur as supreme among warriors, tales presenting him as a sort of fairy-tale potentate with a vast array of followers— Geoffrey makes little use of that; and it tells us almost nothing historically, apart perhaps from a couple of allusions to Arthur as 'emperor', which, to judge from Irish usage, may be equivalent to 'high king'. He is introduced as a king, in a rather uncertain sense, in a few legends of Welsh saints. But all this is nebulous. After Geoffrey, of course, romance takes him over from the Celts and makes him not only king of Britain but even, ironically, king of *England*, losing touch with reality almost entirely.

Scholars who have tried to get at a 'historical Arthur' have swept Geoffrey aside and focused on the *Historia Brittonum* and the *Annales Cambriae*. But these, though closer to Arthur's reputed lifetime, were still written centuries after it; they already have legendary touches that call them in question; and they raise insoluble problems over date, spreading out his warriorship over eighty or ninety years. By singling out different bits of evidence he can be reconstructed in different ways, and the mutual contradictions are daunting. He has been 'found' not only in the West Country but in Wales and the north, many thinking the last to be likeliest. He has been portrayed as anything from a petty local chief to an emperor in the Roman manner proclaimed in Britain. Conversely, he has been consigned to non-existence by rejecting the evidence altogether. It seems clear that while some of the Welsh testimony may be true, it cannot prove his reality by itself, or locate his home territory.

Most people who have sifted this early matter have still been inclined to judge that there is a real person lurking behind it somewhere, a leader of the Britons who made a deep impression, remembered and glorified and made a patriotic symbol. Arthur's name is a Welsh form of the Roman *Artorius*, and could very well have belonged to a real person born in the early post-imperial time when Britons were still giving their children Roman names. It certainly doesn't suggest a Celtic god or mythical hero. Further, there is a sudden wave of Arthurs in the sixth century, as if a man so named, living not vastly long before, had become a popular character in song and story. The folklorist Jennifer Westwood has made an interesting point about the legend of Arthur lying asleep in a cave, as he does at Cadbury. The same is told of other national heroes, such as the German emperor Frederick, and the cave-sleeper is always or nearly always a real person, the legend seldom or never attaches itself to anyone imaginary. Therefore by inference Arthur is a real person.

But none of this gives him definite historical substance, and four-fifths of Geoffrey's account of him, including the most important parts, has no Welsh antecedents anyway. The Welsh trail may not be a totally false one—I don't believe it is, myself—but it doesn't lead to a provable Arthur-figure or a satisfactory candidate for the lordship of Cadbury. Strangely, however, Geoffrey's fantasy does, if we go back to it and start in another direction.

A KING EMERGING

Archaeology is archaeology. It is risky to connect its findings with individuals, as Heinrich Schliemann did when he dug up a golden mask in Greece and announced that he had gazed on the face of Agamemnon. At Cadbury, nevertheless, it is fair to ask whether the documentation of the crumbling Empire offers a candidate for the role of refortifier. It does.

I came across him—or at least, resumed my acquaintance with him, because I had noticed him long before—when searching for Geoffrey's sources of information. It had impressed me that Geoffrey devoted half his narrative of Arthur to the King's warfare in Gaul. Assessed by allocation of space, his Arthur is more a Gallic conqueror than anything else. Yet scholars had nearly always dismissed this side of him as pure fiction. Arthur couldn't have had anything to do with the continent, not really. So they looked for pre-Geoffrey traces of him only in Britain, which meant in practice only among the Welsh; and the Welsh matter is inconclusive.

But, as I said, the idea that Geoffrey merely invented such an enormous portion of the story is contrary to his method of working throughout his *History*, from Julius Caesar to the post-Arthurian close. He claims in a preface to have used 'a certain very ancient book written in the British language.' No such book exists, and the claim isn't believable in the way he states it, but he could have had some lost work besides the Welsh matter—in Breton, perhaps?—and that could have given him whatever he blew up into Arthur's Gallic campaigning.

I spotted a remarkable fact. One of the difficulties with the Welsh Arthur is that we never get a chronological fix for him. We do get a few discrepant dates, but they hang in a void, they never line him up with known history outside Britain. Nobody ever says that he became king when So-and-so was emperor or that he passed away when So-and-so was pope. But Geoffrey does give a chronological fix, the only one that Arthur gets anywhere up to his time, and it comes in the neglected Gallic story. Three times he says that when Arthur was in Gaul, Leo was emperor. This would be Leo I, who ruled at Constantinople, over the eastern part of the Empire, in 457–74. There are other pointers of the same sort, less certain but consistent, that narrow the time-span down, perhaps as closely as the years 469–70.

These clues led me straight to real documents, revealing a real British king whose career Geoffrey could have read about and could have been using in his portrayal of Arthur. More exciting possibly, and some may think more important, is the fact that he could have been the king who refortified Cadbury. Indeed he is not simply a candidate, he is the only one with serious documentation. That is not decisive when we have so little documentation of any kind, but the case for him definitely carries weight.

Across the Channel, where we catch sight of him, the situation in the 460s was chaotic. Gaul was still officially Roman, but large pieces of it were occupied by barbarians and semi-barbarians. Some, such as the Burgundians, were friendly to the Empire, others were not. Euric, king of the Visigoths, had conquered much of Spain and was threatening to overrun Gaul from the south. Leo I, at Constantinople, appointed a western colleague named Anthemius who tried to check the Visigoths by a British alliance. In 468 a man described as the King of the Britons crossed over to Gaul, bringing, it is said, 12,000 ship-borne troops. He was in the country a year or more and advanced to Bourges and beyond, but Gaul's imperial prefect, the emperor's deputy-ruler, undermined him by treacherous dealings with the Visigoths. The Britons were defeated, no imperial forces having come to their aid, and their king escaped with the remains of his army into the nearby country of the Burgundians. No more is heard of him. But there is no doubt as to his reality. We even have a letter to him—absolutely contemporary evidence.

Until lately few historians took much notice of him, owing to a notion that he was merely a chief of Bretons, meaning people of British stock occupying the north-west corner of Gaul in the region then called Armorica. Britons did settle that region and convert it into Brittany, and a trickle of colonists had probably begun during the 450s, but not enough had arrived by 468 to field an army with any prospect of standing up to the Visigoths. In any case a Breton army would not have travelled by sea, being on the continent already. Two recent historians, James Campbell and Ian Wood, confess to finding this 'King of the Britons' puzzling but accept that he started out from Britain. In Professor Campbell's eyes he is credible as 'a British ruler having authority on both sides of the Channel'. The probable context was that British action against the Saxons in the island, perhaps under Ambrosius's generalship, had been successful enough to contain them and dispel any misgivings about taking troops overseas. The king judged the home front to be secure and worked in concert with Rome, as the record states, to stop the barbarians in Gaul as they had been stopped in Britain.

With slight spelling variations he is referred to by continental writers as not only the King of the Britons but Riothamus. What has been realized only in recent years is that this is not his name. It Latinizes a title or honorific in the British language, *Rigotamos*, which would have meant 'supreme king' or 'supremely royal'. History supplies quite a number of cases of rulers being referred to in such a way, rather than by their own names. For instance, a Mongol conqueror named Temujin is always known by his adopted title Genghis Khan, 'Very Mighty Ruler'. The style 'Riothamus' means much the same as 'Vortigern' and suggests that the man in question was at least nominally another high king, perhaps Vortigern's successor. Thus he fits in well with what has been conjectured about the lord of Cadbury, and, in view of the progressive break-up of post-Roman Britain, it would be increasingly hard to imagine anyone later who would.

One further point. His accessibility to the Roman contact, and his cross-Channel activity, suggest that his own domain extended over the West Country, close to the appropriate sea-routes. Whatever Britain's political map in the 460s (so far as there was one), all this area, at the earliest date when we do know what was happening, comprises a single kingdom—Dumnonia—including Somerset and therefore including Cadbury. His army proves that he had the resources of manpower for the great refortification.

The last question here of course is whether this King of the Britons with an unknown name actually was Arthur, the authentic original. This is a separate question from the archaeological one, but if the answer were to be 'yes', the threads at Cadbury-Camelot could be drawn felicitously together. In a qualified sense I am willing to maintain that he was. 'Arthur'—Artorius—may or may not have been his name, we have no way of telling. But a Breton writer in (probably) the eleventh century, giving a sketch of this period, mentions the Gallic war of a leader whom he calls both 'the King of the Britons' and 'Arthur'. For him at any rate they are the same person. When we return to Geoffrey, if we compare his book with the Breton's, the impression is that both draw on an older history, closer to the events. His references to the emperor Leo are not the sole reason for thinking that he has Riothamus in mind in his narrative of Arthur in Gaul. While, as is his habit, he inflates and exaggerates and soars off into flights of fancy, changing the nature of the war for the King's greater glory, a surprising number of passages look as if they were prompted by this one episode.

Riothamus, the King of the Britons, led an army through Gaul, not only in the reign of Leo but during the exact years which Geoffrey's other hints indicate. He advanced to the neighbourhood of Burgundy. He was betrayed by a deputy-ruler who conspired with barbarians. He fades from our view after a fatal battle. His last continental location is among the Burgundians, and his line of retreat shows him moving in the direction of the real Burgundian town of Avallon. Finally, he has no recorded death. All these features of his career have echoes in Geoffrey's *History*, and even the out-of-line date for Arthur's passing, 542, could have been arrived at by recognized forms of error (though I won't go into it here) from 470, the probable date of Riothamus's 'passing'. The King of the Britons, besides being the only documented candidate as the royal refortifier, is the only documented person who does anything Arthurian.

He supplies a basis for much more of Geoffrey's account than the Welsh matter does—fully half. As we have no record of him in Britain before he took his army abroad, we have no way to decide whether the Welsh matter may also derive from him. He could certainly have fought some of the battles ascribed to Arthur, all the locatable ones, in fact. Others he could not. King Arthur may very well be a composite figure created by a gradual blending of several heroes, real or imaginary. Many would urge that there is a strong case for a northern one. Even so I suspect that it was a process of grafting other men's deeds on to a single famous original, and that the king who went to Gaul was the starting-point of the Arthurian Legend and can legitimately be called Arthur-Riothamus.

If we want to picture him, he would have been at least nominally a Christian, bi-lingual in Latin and the British language, literate, with something like a classical education. While knights in full medieval armour are out of the question, a personal following of cavalry of Late Roman type would be possible, though with limited effectiveness, because the stirrup had not yet reached western Europe. As for Guinevere, I will give some consideration to her further on.*

* The Arthur–Riothamus question is a complex one raising many issues. I have discussed them with suitable references in *Speculum*, the journal of the Medieval Academy of America (April 1981); in a book, *The Discovery of King Arthur*; and in several contributions to the *Arthurian Encyclopedia* published by Garland, New York.

4. The Shifting Scene~ Places and People

BRENT KNOLL

MORE THAN ONCE I have mentioned Brent Knoll. It is near Berrow on the coast of the Bristol Channel, visible all the way from Cadbury when the weather is clear, and from Glastonbury Tor, which is between, at most times. The Knoll is another isolated hill, bare and grassy, 450 feet high. A Celtic settlement in pre-Roman days created defences like the earthworks of Cadbury but a great deal simpler. One rampart only, and one ditch only, girdle the summit area. The hillside below is steep, and the ancient occupants, doubtless to discourage attackers, made parts of it steeper.

The name 'Brent' is probably derived from a British word *brigantia* and conveys a notion of height. Brigantia was the name of a British goddess, the High One. Rivers called Brent may have been sacred to her. Brent Knoll, however, is likely to have been called so simply as the high point in this part of Somerset, rising sharply from low and level country. Dion Fortune put it in her novel *The Sea Priestess* thinly disguised as Bell Knowle, suggesting it was a sacred mount indeed, artificially moulded into shape by colonists from Atlantis. Less sensational is the idea that it was a signal-station in a chain linking it with Glastonbury Tor and Cadbury on the one side, and Dinas Powys near Cardiff, from which the Knoll can be sighted, on the other.

This bit of country used to belong to Glastonbury Abbey. A thirteenth-century chronicler justifies its title with a story of King Arthur himself. While holding court at Caerleon over Christmas, he knighted a bold young man named Ider, the son of King Nuth. I am not sure who Nuth was, or what he was king of. He may be the same as Nudd, the father of Gwyn, Glastonbury Tor's uncanny resident. Nudd in turn was originally the god Nodons, who had a temple at Lydney in the Forest of Dean. But Sir Ider emerges from the mists as a human character.

Brent Knoll, Somerset. A hill-fort where a legend of three giants may be a relic of the belief that beings of huge size were responsible for prehistoric earthworks and megaliths.

His accolade had to be confirmed by a test. When Arthur was at Glastonbury he told Ider of three giants 'notorious for their wickedness' who lived on Brent Knoll, which was then known as the Mount of Frogs. He would march against them and Ider must join the party. Ider over-zealously galloped ahead and slew all three single-handed. When Arthur caught up, he found the giant-killer lying unconscious and apparently dead or dying. The King returned sadly to Glastonbury blaming himself, appointed some monks to pray for Ider's soul, and endowed the Abbey with lands around the hill.

It seems, however, that he acted too hastily in assuming Ider's death. To judge from other stories the knight survived. With his name spelt Yder, he comes into the tale of *Erec* by the French poet Chrétien de Troyes, and another Frenchman gives him a whole romance to himself. This tells of his love for the lady Guenloie. He undertook adventures in true knightly style to prove himself worthy of her. Impressed by his exploits in a siege, where he was treacherously wounded, she nursed him back to health. Arthur enrolled him in the Round Table. When he killed a bear that had wandered into Guinevere's bedroom, she was understandably grateful, but Arthur suspected that her feelings went beyond gratitude, and pushed her into admitting that if she were to marry again she would choose Ider. The atmosphere grew strained. All ended happily, however. In this version the giant-killing is a test imposed by Guenloie, and when Ider passes it she marries him.

There are hints that Ider was once actually reputed to be Guinevere's lover, though the author of this particular tale thinks otherwise, and disapproves of the King's jealous conduct. He has unexpected touches of realism, as when another married lady makes advances to Ider and he kicks her in the stomach. Chivalry, even fictitious chivalry, was not always as chivalrous as you might suppose.

DUNSTER

I once gave a course on matters Arthurian at an American university. After it had been going for several weeks, a student complained that he had expected giants and dragons and wasn't getting them. Somerset provides giants at Brent Knoll, and it provides a dragon of sorts at Dunster. Also, for good measure, a castle.

Dunster is on a hillside at the approaches of Exmoor, three miles southeast of Minehead. The castle is of mixed date. Its oldest surviving portion is a gateway built in the thirteenth century. But there was a Norman stronghold before that, and a Celtic one before that, either on the present site or possibly a little way inland, where Bat's Castle is a recognizable hill-fort. The original Dunster fort, at whichever place, may have been Irish rather than British. Irish settlers were in possession of parts of Wales in the early post-Roman period, and were frequenting Somerset, if not living there in large numbers, for a long time afterwards. Irish writers speak of Glastonbury in almost proprietary tones as 'Glastonbury of the Gaels', because of its shrines of St Patrick and St Brigit and pilgrimages to these, and the prominence of Irish monks at its school, where they pioneered the process of improving the Abbey's early history. One of the texts that refer to these topics refers also to a 'three-fossed' fort that once belonged to an Irish prince, and this may be Dunster.

Whether an Irishman took it over from previous Britons, or Britons took it over from him, or both, or neither, it figures as a British place in a list of this island's twenty-eight cities attached to the *Historia Brittonum* of 'Nennius', where it stands twenty-fourth. The Welsh name is Dindraithov or Dindraethou. Its Arthur story comes into one of several 'lives' of saints that mention him. They were composed at the monastery of Llancarfan near Barry. We have already noticed one of them, Caradoc's 'life' of Gildas, telling of the kidnapping and rescue of Guinevere. These works are mainly legend, not real biography, but they give us glimpses of the Llancarfan monks' attitudes to Arthur, which were a good deal short of hero-worship.

The Dunster story is in the 'life' of St Carannog. He is stated to have been a grandson, or great-grandson, of a northern chieftain named Cunedda who reputedly moved to Wales with his large family, and was put in charge there by Britain's last Roman rulers or first independent ones. While Cunedda may or may not have existed, there is no special reason to doubt that Carannog did, though we need not believe all we are told about him.

His 'life' relates that he had a portable altar with unusual properties. No one could decide what colour it was, and it floated. He launched it into the Severn estuary, resolving to preach wherever it landed, and it drifted down the Bristol Channel and ran aground near Dunster. Here Arthur presided jointly with a certain Cato or Cadwy, as a junior partner it seems, since the writer mentions Cato first. Cato, or Cadwy, may have been an ancestor of the British kings who ruled the West Country—Dumnonia—before its absorption into Wessex. Perhaps this was an early phase of Arthur's career. Anyhow, when Carannog arrived, the altar was nowhere to be seen, but Arthur was. He was trying without success to catch a gigantic serpent that was ravaging the district. Carannog asked about the altar, and Arthur replied that he would reveal where it was if the saint would prove his sanctity by getting rid of the serpent. Celtic holy men were apt to be good at this kind of thing, the major instance being St Patrick, who, it will be remembered, banished all the snakes from Ireland.

Carannog prayed, and the monster slithered noisily to his feet in submission. He put his stole round its neck and it followed him, lifting neither its wings nor its talons (clearly it belonged to the dragon class), into the hall of the fortress. There Carannog gave it something to eat in the presence of Cato and the court. A cry went up for its death, but he said it had been divinely sent to destroy sinners, and banished it with a stern warning to behave itself. When the serpent was safely out of the way, Arthur produced the missing altar. He had taken it himself, and tried to use it as a table, but, resenting the sacrilege, it had tossed off everything he put on it, and he was not sorry to see it go. In reparation he made Carannog a gift of land at 'Carrum' to build a church on, and subsequently another for the same purpose at 'Carrou' where a stream runs into the sea just east of Watchet.

Carrum is Carhampton near the seaside resort of Blue Anchor, and the story is meant to explain how its church's land became ecclesiastical property. Carhampton's original name was indeed Carrum, and it was an identified place a long time ago. A battle was fought here in 836 against a horde of Danish pirates. However, the name is not a shortened form of 'Carannog', though the Welsh writer may intend his readers to think so. It comes from an Anglo-Saxon word meaning a rock.

An interesting aspect of the Carannog legend is that it locates Arthur where it does. This is in keeping with the testimony of Wales in general. It was the Britons' Welsh descendants, the Llancarfan monks among them, who handed down Arthur's saga. Yet although the Welsh claimed him as theirs, they pictured him as living outside Wales, which he entered as a visitor or to hold court but not as his homeland. In the 'life' of Gildas, when Guinevere is at Glastonbury, Arthur comes to her rescue with troops from Devon and Cornwall, not Wales. In the 'life' of Carannog he is in Somerset again. Other Welsh traditions give him a Cornish residence called Kelliwic. And while the tale of his birth at Tintagel—or at any rate his begetting—is due to Geoffrey, the Welsh never seriously offer a birthplace to rival it, any more than they offer a grave to rival the one at Glastonbury.

To Cornwall then I turn . . .

TINTAGEL

Tintagel (pronounced Tin-TAJ-el) is the one great Arthurian spectacular, the scene of Arthur's legendary conception and, it is normally assumed, his birth. You approach it over uplands in North Cornwall where trees bend sideways from the prevailing wind. Because of the way the coastline runs, this area does not face across the Bristol Channel but into the open Atlantic, and at some points you can look straight out to sea with nothing between yourself and North America.

Tintagel village lies slightly inland and, regrettably, is the single place where the Arthurian Legend has produced a tourist trap. We need not dwell on phenomena like King Arthur's Car Park. At the seaward end of the narrow street, beside a shop selling postcards, paperbacks, and other matter for visitors, a track leads down into a ravine, one of several along this rocky coast. The ravine was used for a battle in MGM's first wide-screen film, *The Knights of the Round Table*, and local promoters have annexed the name 'Vale of Avalon', but on no acceptable grounds.

Leaving the village behind and out of sight, you can walk down the ravine along the track, which is steep at first but becomes easier. In the tourist season a Land-Rover service shuttles back and forth. A swift stream tumbles along beside the track, finally plunging over a little cliff as a waterfall, and entering the sea.

This is the spectacular part. As you stand facing outwards where the stream goes over the edge, you have a high rocky headland on your right and another on your left. Below, in between, is a cove which has a sandy beach at low tide. A path running off to your left divides into two stairways. One goes down to the cove, the other goes up towards the promontory on that side, which is the Arthurian one.

It is almost an island, and rises 250 feet above the sea. The isthmus or ridge joining it to the mainland was once higher but, in historical times, never wide. Long ago it crumbled and left a chasm, once spanned by a drawbridge, now by a bridge that stays in position. Steep flights of steps go up to two portions of a ruined castle, one on the hill on the mainland side, the other out on the headland. The latter is the important part.

Here is the story. According to Geoffrey of Monmouth in his *History*, Arthur's father was Uther, Pendragon or 'foremost leader' as he was styled, the younger of two brothers who reigned in Britain after Vortigern's downfall. When exactly? With Geoffrey exactitude is rare, but one of his few good dates for this period, defined by what I call a chronological fix, is 429. At that time Vortigern, infatuated with the daughter of the Saxon chief Hengist, makes a fatal deal handing over Kent to her heathen father. Saxon treacheries and aggressions follow in short order. Vortigern perishes under siege in the hill-fort of Little Doward near Monmouth. Uther's brother Aurelius Ambrosius reigns briefly but is murdered, and Uther succeeds him, with the Saxons more or less held but not conquered. Geoffrey has made the Saxon eruption swifter and therefore earlier than it was, with the result that Uther's reign seems to belong to the 430s and 40s. This fits fairly well—not perfectly, but fairly—with later indications of date for the reign of Uther's mighty son.

Arthur, the national saviour, is the fruit of another royal amour which, so to speak, cancels out Vortigern's. Geoffrey relates how the newly crowned Uther held court in London at Easter, when his eye fell upon Ygerna, the beautiful wife of Gorlois, Duke of Cornwall. He was smitten with ungovernable desire for her, and paid her so much attention at a banquet that it was soon obvious. He kept sending attendants to her with plates of food and goblets of wine, and 'engaged her in sprightly conversation'. When the conversation became too sprightly her husband decided that enough was enough. He left without asking the King's leave and took Ygerna with him. Uther treated the discourtesy as an insult and led troops to Cornwall to ravage the ducal lands.

Gorlois had to arm his own retainers and make what resistance he could. For Ygerna's safety he immured her in his castle on the Tintagel headland, since a few guards could hold the narrow approach against an army. He then occupied a fortified camp at Dimilioc, which, to judge from the Domesday survey, was St Dennis twenty-odd miles away. St Dennis lies south of Goss Moor between Newquay and St Austell. Gorlois's fort would have been on a steep conical hill north of the town. A church surmounts it today, but the churchyard wall marks the line of the old fortifications, and indeed this may originally have been the church of the *dinas*, meaning the stronghold, the saint's name 'Dennis' being a misunderstanding.

Uther marched down to Dimilioc and laid siege. However, he was so obsessed with thoughts of Ygerna that he could not concentrate. Ulfin, a confidant of his, pointed out the difficulty of getting to her inside Tintagel, and suggested consulting Merlin. The enchanter had come to Cornwall in the royal retinue, doubtless with foresight of what would happen, and he was equal to the occasion. He produced a potion that turned Uther into an exact replica of the lady's husband, and Ulfin into a replica of a friend of his, a member of the castle staff at Tintagel. Merlin changed his own appearance as well. The trio made their way to Tintagel at sundown and were let in, since no one suspected that the leader was not Gorlois. Thus, in the most effective disguise imaginable, Uther reached Ygerna. In the character of her husband he pretended to have left Dimilioc to make sure all was well at Tintagel. He had his way with her and she conceived Arthur.

Meanwhile, back at Dimilioc, Gorlois had made an ill-advised sortie and fallen in battle. The fighting was over. Messengers hurried to Tintagel with the news, and were bewildered to find a man who appeared to be Gorlois sitting beside Ygerna. The disguised Uther assured them they were mistaken, but slipped away on the pretext of peace negotiations, resumed his own appearance, and checked that Gorlois was dead. Then he married Ygerna. In view of the course of events on the crucial night, her son's paternity was in no doubt, and he was the heir to the kingdom.

I wonder whether the implications of this tale are always grasped. In the film *Excalibur*, Uther wears full medieval armour. A suit of that kind weighed fifty or sixty pounds. Thus accoutred, he would have had to scale a long, steep flight of steps to get to the castle. After doing so, one would think, it might be some time before a climber felt equal to amorous activity. In the film, nevertheless, Uther not only proceeds but assails Ygerna still wearing his suit of armour, complete even with the helmet. It would have been hard on her.

Perhaps, when Geoffrey chose this location, the connecting ridge was so much higher that the final approach wouldn't have raised that precise problem. But he certainly had it in mind that the approach was narrow, if less laborious. What else did he have in mind? The medieval castle does not go back to the fifth century or anywhere near. Its founder was Reginald, Earl of Cornwall. Geoffrey dedicated his *History* to a half-brother of Reginald and could have set the episode here partly to please the two noblemen. The objection is that the castle was not started till 1141, or a year or two later, whereas

Geoffrey finished the *History* in or before 1138. The present version may be a second edition, with Tintagel inserted only after Reginald's builders began work, but there is no evidence for such a drastic rehandling of one of the most important episodes. On the face of it, when Geoffrey wrote his account of Arthur's origin, he chose a place where nothing was visible to make it appropriate. Yet singling out a bare and bleak promontory for a completely imaginary stronghold is not like him.

Beyond the castle ruins, however, fresh possibilities open up. Along the headland's precipitous sides, and above on its comparatively level top, are stone enclosures. These are restorations of the remains of buildings unearthed by Ralegh Radford during the 1930s. It was in and around them that he came across the imported pottery which was later to draw attention to Cadbury. Expensive ware for holding expensive stuff, it was brought from the eastern Mediterranean, perhaps also from North Africa, and proved occupation by a wealthy household in the fifth or sixth century, or, of course, both. At the date of discovery, hardly anything was known of this period in western Britain, and it was doubtful how the site should be interpreted. Radford favoured a Celtic monastery, and explained various buildings as a chapel, a guest-house, and so on. But work on other sites has made it more likely that the pottery was refuse from a princely residence which he never found, or never identified. Tintagel may have been a considerable settlement.

Like Leland at Cadbury, Geoffrey apparently got hold of a tradition of the place's importance at about the right time, and this, coupled with the topography, determined his choice. It is obviously interesting that he looked to Cornwall at all when he might have been expected to prefer Wales. He surely had a strong, even compelling historical reason for launching Arthur's career where he did. Just after the episode he has an intriguing touch that could point in the same direction, if very differently. When Uther married Ygerna, he tells us, they 'lived together as equals'. This is one of several hints, dropped by Geoffrey and other medieval authors, at a lingering awareness of the old Celtic scheme of things in which a queen was far more than a mere consort or appendage. There will be more to say about this in connection with Guinevere. When I reviewed a book that dealt with the subject, my article appeared in a national newspaper under the headline WOMEN'S LIB RULED IN ARTHUR'S CAMELOT.

The plateau on top of Tintagel's headland is open and windswept. Rock formations around the sides have names like Arthur's Chair and Arthur's Cups and Saucers. Towards the highest area is a curious tunnel of unknown purpose. Far below is the cove. The proper time for a foray down there is when the tide is out, partly because the beach dwindles away at high water, partly because of Merlin's Cave, which passes right through the sea-swept base of the castle promontory. Mary Stewart in her novel *The Crystal Cave* has another in mind, but this one claims to be haunted by Merlin's ghost. At low

Tintagel, Cornwall. Merlin's Cave under the castle promontory, looking out through the entrance on to the cove where, in Tennyson's poem, the infant Arthur is washed ashore.

tide you can enter it from the beach and pass through. The floor is tricky and full of pools, and you will get your feet wet and maybe slip, but the walk is rewarding, and brings you out into daylight through an opening at the far end, among a cluster of massive rocks. The opening is at a lower level than the entrance in the cove, so that as the tide rises, the sea flows in from that end and surges gradually up through the cave, with roarings and moanings and deluges of spray, till it blocks the entrance.

Across the beach is the other headland, Barras Nose. This too has a cave, which is more difficult to follow the whole way, but goes through like Merlin's. I have never heard any legends about it, and for a long time the only person I ever met who knew it went through was a waitress in San Francisco named Wilma. So I call it Wilma's Cave.

To revert to Uther and Ygerna, the motif of a substituted sexual partner occurs in other contexts, even in Shakespeare. Accepted once as a story-telling convention, it scarcely carries conviction now. However closely the man who came to Ygerna resembled her husband, she would have sensed something wrong, especially if he gave such a weak explanation. Novelists retelling the tale have preferred to suggest some kind of collusion. Tennyson, in his *Idylls of the King*, saw Arthur's origin as a problem more than a hundred years ago, if not for quite the same reason. Whether or not magic could be stretched to make the scene credible, it was too scandalous for his taste and he offered alternatives, one of them being that Arthur's advent was magical in a more awe-inspiring sense. In *The Coming of Arthur*, Bleys, Merlin's master, is reported as telling how Uther died childless at Tintagel when he and Merlin were there. They 'left the still King', walked outside for fresh air, and then...

> ...from the castle gateway by the chasm
> Descending thro' the dismal night—a night
> In which the bounds of heaven and earth were lost—
> Beheld, so high upon the dreary deeps
> It seem'd in heaven, a ship, the shape thereof
> A dragon wing'd, and all from stem to stern
> Bright with a shining people on the decks,
> And gone as soon as seen. And then the two
> Dropt to the cove, and watch'd the great sea fall,
> Wave after wave, each mightier than the last,
> Till last, a ninth one, gathering half the deep
> And full of voices, slowly rose and plunged
> Roaring, and all the wave was in a flame:
> And down the wave and in the flame was borne

Opposite
Tintagel, Cornwall. Merlin's Cave, looking out towards the far end, where the sea floods in as the tide rises.

> A naked babe, and rode to Merlin's feet,
> Who stoopt and caught the babe, and cried 'The King!
> Here is an heir for Uther!' and the fringe
> Of that great breaker, sweeping up the strand,
> Lash'd at the wizard as he spake the word,
> And all at once all round him rose in fire,
> So that the child and he were clothed in fire.
> And presently thereafter follow'd calm,
> Free sky and stars.

By giving Arthur such a mysterious origin, Tennyson is balancing his mysterious end; though the mystery is compounded by the report's being second-hand with no guarantee of truth. A few lines later Merlin says enigmatically: 'From the great deep to the great deep he goes.' But you can tread in Merlin's footsteps as Tennyson did, 'from the castle gateway by the chasm' down to the cove. And you can 'watch the great sea fall', though I have never been convinced that the ninth wave is larger.

What happened afterwards? Gorlois being dead, someone else was heir to his domain and his castle. The next Duke of Cornwall whom Geoffrey mentions is Cador. He is probably the same as that Cadwy whom the tale of Carannog locates at Dunster, in Arthur's company (the dates don't really work, but who cares?). Geoffrey never states Cador's relation to the deceased Gorlois, but I think he is a younger brother. When Arthur is King, Cador has an honoured role in court ceremonial, and shows himself a fine leader in war, brave, loyal and good-humoured. His son Constantine, Arthur's cousin, succeeds to the crown after the King's passing and takes vengeance on the sons of the traitor Mordred.

Long before that, according to Geoffrey, Duke Cador did something else. He took Guinevere into his household as a child and brought her up. This is where we first hear of her in Geoffrey's account. He says she was descended from a noble Roman family, but gives no clue as to how she found her way into a Cornish foster-home. Romancers who enlarge on her background tell us that her father was Leodegan, 'king' of Carmelide or Camelerd, a name that may echo the Cornish river Camel and the town of Camelford on its banks. They also tell us that he owned the Round Table before Arthur. Merlin made it for Uther, who passed it on to Leodegan, and it came to Arthur as Guinevere's dowry when he married her. Merlin foresaw trouble, but the marriage proceeded.

The old form of her name is Gwenhwyfar, meaning the White Phantom. Welsh tradition is unkind to her, dubbing her the most faithless of women. In Wales, till quite recently, it was a reflection on a girl's virtue to call her a Guinevere. Arthur's Queen does have a penchant for involvement, willing or unwilling, with men other than her husband, though her long amour with the splendid Lancelot finally dominates, and little more is heard of anyone else.

My own feeling is that the Cornish connection is unconvincing, and Guinevere makes more sense as a northern princess. As with Uther and Ygerna, her case may recall the old Celtic queenship, but in a more controversial aspect. The Celtic queen, free and equal, could take lovers as a king could take concubines. By the time the story of such a queen reached medieval story-tellers, moral ideas had altered and they could not understand it. Guinevere with her lover Lancelot was viewed as disloyal and unfaithful. Yet enough of the reality still persisted to give the triangular situation an unusual quality. The royal affair goes on for years, Arthur turns a blind eye so long as it remains discreet, and (a rarity in literature) although he is cuckolded, this never lowers his stature or makes him ridiculous. As for the geography, Lancelot's home is in the north beyond the Humber, and the great historical precedent is Cartimandua, a British queen during the first century who tried to preserve the north's independence by friendship with Rome. Cartimandua had a lover. She managed the policy, and her own triangular situation, till she divorced her husband to marry the favourite. Thereupon the husband, in a vindictive flurry of pseudo-patriotism, turned against her Roman allies and the north was attacked and overrun.

To return, though, to Cornwall and Tintagel. Legend detaches the castle of Arthurian times from any sort of reality. It is said to have been built by giants, to have been painted in a chequer design of green and blue, to have been invisible on two days of the year. All this can be set aside. More important is its reappearance in the romance of Tristan and Isolde (to adopt Wagner's spelling), where it becomes a residence of King Mark of Cornwall, Isolde's husband. I don't know of any explanation. Speculate, if you like, that Cador resigned his Cornish domain to serve Arthur at court, and Mark took the stronghold over. But the Wagnerian drama has to be looked at separately, in other settings.

LYONESSE

Tristan, or Tristram, is a hero whose adventures have drawn in legendary themes from several parts of the British Isles, even from the far-off land of the Picts. While the main locale is in Cornwall, opinions differ as to whether the story started there. Tristan is said to have been a son of the ruler of Lyonesse. That fails to settle the question, because of a doubt as to where Lyonesse was originally supposed to be. Early romancers who tell of him may be thinking of Lothian in Scotland, called Loenois in Old French, or Leonais in Brittany. Today, however, the place is part of Cornish mythology, as Tristan himself is.

Lyonesse is a land engulfed by the ocean. You can see where it reputedly was from the coasts around Cornwall's south-west extremities. It was a low-lying region stretching all the way to the Isles of Scilly, and around towards

A Neolithic tomb on St Mary's in the Isles of Scilly, which have many traces of early inhabitants. Folk-memories of the islands' past went into the making of the legend of Lyonesse.

the Lizard, so that Mount's Bay did not exist. Lyonesse had several towns and 140 churches. When the sea swept over it, no one knows when, a man named Trevilian jumped on a white horse, rode madly to Perranuthnoe near Marazion, and sheltered in a cave to watch the inundation. The Trevelyan family's coat of arms shows a horse emerging from water. Fishermen used to claim that the Seven Stones reef off Land's End marked the site of one of the vanished towns, the City of Lions, and that they hauled up fragments of masonry in their nets. As in other places with legends of this kind, church bells are allegedly heard under water when the weather is rough.

Various folk-memories, picturesquely exaggerated, have gone into the tale. Some of the Isles of Scilly were joined together in the last centuries BC, and as late as Roman times, till the sea divided them. Walls and huts lie below the present high-water mark. An islet called Great Arthur witnesses to a legendary link with the King. Round the mainland coast in Mount's Bay are fossil remains of a sunken forest, with beech trees still bearing nuts. The Cornish name for St Michael's Mount, the steep-sided island opposite Marazion, is *Carrick luz en cuz*, 'the ancient rock in the wood'. Stone axes dating from the second millennium BC have been drawn up from the sea-bed. Not only was it dry land, it had inhabitants.

While Tristan can hardly have been a prince of a mini-Atlantis, his milieu in this part of Britain is not pure fantasy. Nor, as we shall see, is Mark's. The tragic love-story has been handled by a medley of authors, in a variety of ways, but in substance it is this.

Tristan was a nephew of King Mark of Cornwall. The King of Ireland claimed tribute from Cornwall, and sent over his wife's brother Morholt to enforce the demand. Morholt, a massive and formidable warrior, agreed to settle the issue by single combat. Tristan came forward as Cornwall's champion, and killed him. A splinter of Tristan's sword broke off, lodging in Morholt's skull and remaining there when the body was taken home.

Tristan later went to Ireland himself. He was identified as Morholt's slayer by the splinter's fitting into his sword, but he appeased the wrath of the Irish royal couple by other deeds. They had a daughter named Isolde (I will stick here to the spelling familiarized by Wagner, but, as with most of these legendary names, there are several). Isolde was skilful in healing arts and cured Tristan when he was wounded fighting a dragon. She consented to marry his uncle Mark, but while Tristan was escorting her to Cornwall they accidentally drank a potion she was meant to share with her bridegroom, and fell hopelessly and eternally in love.

The marriage proceeded nevertheless, and they both lived at King Mark's court, at Tintagel and elsewhere. In a furtive relationship they passed through many episodes of anguish and bliss, shame and joy. For a long time Mark was never sure what was going on. Courtiers who knew tried to convince him, but the lovers succeeded in throwing him off the scent and sometimes he persuaded himself that they were blameless. At last, however, he was forced to face the truth. Tristan went into exile.

In Brittany he met another Isolde and married her, but the old passion never expired and the marriage remained nominal. Wounded again, he sent a message to the Irish Isolde begging her to come over and cure him. He was uncertain whether she would. It was arranged that the expected ship would carry white sails if she was aboard and black ones if not. When Tristan's Breton wife sighted the ship approaching, she saw that the sails were white, but jealously told him they were black. He died of despair, and when Isolde arrived she died also, grief-stricken. Mark allowed them to be buried side by side at Tintagel. A vine grew from Tristan's grave and a rose-tree from Isolde's, and the branches intertwined.

When this tale was told first, it stood in its own right and was not part of any larger scheme. But even in the earliest surviving written versions King Arthur is already present playing a marginal role or at least mentioned. As the Arthurian cycle grew more popular, romance drew Tristan fully into it, making him a knight of the Round Table. We read of Lancelot becoming his friend and giving the lovers a haven in his own castle. Tristan is credited with many adventures that confuse the main story and often threaten to swamp it. But even apart from all this elaboration, he is more interesting than most medieval heroes. He is versatile, not just a doughty fighter but a harpist, a singer, a linguist, a chess-player, an expert huntsman. His talents foreshadow the ideals of a later age, the Renaissance.

The grand passion, also, has an interest beyond its tragic power. Medieval romance tells of plenty of amorous affairs, in keeping with the conventions of what was called Courtly Love, but the mutual obsession of Tristan and Isolde may be the first literary instance in Europe of a love portrayed as a law unto itself, overriding all else, and giving a quasi-justification to almost anything that serves its ends. Even apart from the plain fact of adultery, Tristan is grossly disloyal to his king, yet he persists. Isolde is cunning and ruthless, contemplating the murder of her own maid to cover her tracks. She lulls her husband's suspicions with words that are strictly true but ingeniously misleading. Yet through all misconduct and disaster, sympathy seldom fails. In a thirteenth-century poetic version by Gottfried von Strassburg, the chief inspiration of Wagner's opera, the German author makes Isolde undergo a trial by ordeal in which she has to carry a red-hot iron. Christ works a small miracle for her, the iron does not burn, and her innocence is thereby 'proved'.

As for the third member of the triangle, Mark, he passes through an unpleasant change at the hands of successive writers. At first, though not likeable, he has redeeming features, and much of the poignancy of the situation is due to his being wronged more than he has deserved. When the lovers are dead, he learns about the potion and laments that if they had only told him, he would have understood and let Isolde go. But Mark in his later setting as an

Castle Dore, Cornwall.
Interior of the earth-
works. In the enclosure,
excavation revealed
foundations of post-
Roman buildings, favour-
ing a belief that this was a
residence of Kynvawr—in
Latin, Cunomorus, identi-
fied by a ninth-century
writer with King Mark in
the Tristan story.

Arthurian sub-king becomes so base and evil that his nephew and wife seem excusable and the moral tension is weakened. Not only does he kill Tristan, in an altered ending, by stabbing him treacherously with a poisoned spear, he outlives Arthur and lays Camelot waste at the first opportunity.

CASTLE DORE

If we traverse the Cornish peninsula, picking up stretches of the old road that ran from Wadebridge by way of Bodmin to Fowey, we can glimpse the Tristan story in process of formation. Before Gottfried's German poem there was a French one by Béroul, and Béroul steers us towards tangible if enigmatic remains of a far-off past. Among the literary treatments his poem is closest to whatever materials pre-existed, written or oral. It was composed before the end of the twelfth century. Only a long fragment survives, but the fragment has enough in it to show that Béroul, alone among the Tristan romancers, has some real knowledge of the territory. He brings in several Cornish places. Sometimes it is not certain what he has in mind, though a likely guess is usually possible, but he indicates a group of locations where there can be no doubt, and we even find what Arthurian legend never supplies anywhere else, a monument with a name on it.

Though well aware of Tintagel, Béroul gives Mark another home, seemingly a less austere one, which he calls Lancien. This word is a form of Lantyan, and the name still exists. Today it belongs to a farm south of Lostwithiel, and to a nearby wood beside the River Fowey. Also Béroul places an episode at the church of St Samson. Tristan temporarily goes away, and Isolde and Mark have a public reconciliation. She walks with his nobles to the church, is welcomed by monks and other clergy, and lays an embroidered silk robe on the altar as an offering. It is afterwards made into a chasuble, worn only on special occasions, and, Béroul assures us, it is still there. It is not there now, but a church with the right dedication is, St Samson in Golant, on a hillside down the Fowey from Lantyan. The church dates from the fifteenth century, and stands on or near the site of a monastery said to have been founded by St Samson himself, in the sixth. In other words, there was a monastic church here almost early enough to figure in the story. Perhaps not quite early enough, but Béroul is plainly drawing on genuine traditions about the neighbourhood's history.

The road leading into this area is a portion of the old cross-Cornish track, now the B3269, which leaves the A390 near Lostwithiel. As it runs south towards Fowey it passes the present Lantyan and climbs slightly along a ridge. Beside it to the east is a steep bank covered with gorse, and a plaque informs you that Mark lived here. You are still in the medieval manor of Lantyan-in-Golant, still in a place to which Béroul's tradition could apply. A little farther on are some buildings, and a gate on the left leading into a field. You can go through the gate and make your way back along the edge of the field to the aforesaid bank, which you will now recognize as part of a system of earth-works composing a hill-fort like Cadbury, though it does not rise much above the surrounding ground level.

This is Castle Dore. 'Dore' may mean 'golden'—*d'or*—and refer to the golden blossoms on the gorse bushes covering the ramparts. The word 'castle' is used here, as in other cases, of fortifications far earlier than the Middle Ages. Castle Dore has two concentric banks six or seven feet high, both with ditches on the outside. Their last military use was as late as August 1644, when some Roundheads dug in here and a Royalist force evicted them.

Where they adjoin the road the two ramparts are close together, but on the far side the lower one parts company with the higher, extending outwards and leaving a space between, which may have been a yard for animals or a market-place. The entrance to the enclosure, which is 220 feet across, is on that side. Excavations following on from the Tintagel programme revealed that Castle Dore dated from the third century BC. As at Cadbury there was a Celtic settlement inside. As at Cadbury it was vacant during the Roman period, though nothing suggests assault or deportation. As at Cadbury, lastly, it was reoccupied. Work was carried out to refurbish part of the defences, though with nothing like the vast Cadbury restructuring. A cobbled road led in through the entrance, with a small building on a platform beside it, perhaps a guardhouse. Within the enclosure were at least three timber buildings, which could be sketched from patterns of stone-lined holes showing where the sup-porting posts had been. One was 90 feet by 40, with a porch and a hearth, and, to judge from a central row of post-holes, a gabled roof. Another was 65 feet by 35. The floors of these two had been destroyed by ploughing, but patches of stone pavement remained in the fragmentary third building.

Post-Roman Castle Dore did not suggest a new village but a single es-tablishment belonging to a king or regional ruler. Re-founded as such in the fifth century, it continued in occupation for possibly two hundred years. It had a dominant position not only strategically but economically, right beside a main artery of trade and transport with access to the sea at both ends.

But why should the lord of Castle Dore, in the fifth or sixth century, have been Mark? His traditional presence in this area is attested not only by Béroul but by a place near Par Sands a mile or two off, Kilmarth, meaning, in Cornish, Mark's Retreat. Yet Mark is a puzzle, not because too little is said about him, but because too much is. Quite probably he was a real person. His name is Roman like Arthur's, being simply Marcus, and the Welsh give him a father called Marcianus, who may have been named after a fifth-century emperor. The trouble is that Marcianus, if real, was an official or governor in Glamor-gan, and various legends of Mark himself connect him with Wales. The Welsh form of his name is 'March', which unfortunately is Welsh for a horse, and story-tellers exploited the word-play to his disadvantage. In spite of this his fame spread, and not to Cornwall alone.

Mote of Mark, Dumfries and Galloway. A partly fortified hill on the south coast of Scotland, occupied during the sixth century. Its association with Mark is doubtless a later legend, but shows how widely the characters in the Tristan story were known.

Close-up of the Tristan Stone. The letters WORI, running down it, can still be clearly made out. What looks like a W is an inverted M in CUNOMORI, '(son) of Cunomorus'.

The Tristan Stone, near Fowey, Cornwall. A sixth-century monument which has been moved a number of times and was once closer to Castle Dore. Its worn inscription shows that it marked the grave of Drustanus, son of Cunomorus. 'Drustanus' is a form of 'Tristan'. The idea that Cunomorus was the same person as Mark, whether or not correct, underlies the localization of the Tristan-Isolde romance in this part of Cornwall.

On the south coast of Scotland near Rockcliffe, overlooking Rough Firth, is an early fort called Mote of Mark. Like Castle Dore it was occupied during the sixth century. The seaward side fell away sharply to the water, as it still does. On the landward side was a rampart, a drystone wall in a timber frame, one of the few partial British parallels to Cadbury; but it did not go all round and the protected enclosure was far smaller, 200 feet by 130. Inside, excavated fragments of metal and jewellery prove the presence of craftsmen and, by implication, a rich patron. He is most unlikely to have been Mark in person, but if people could even think of Mark in that remote setting, how did he come to be in Cornwall as well?

Part at least of the answer is on the outskirts of Fowey. If you go on past Castle Dore you come to a crossroads, Four Corners. A short distance down the road into Fowey is a lay-by with a much weathered stone monument. It has been moved several times and was formerly closer to Castle Dore. In the course of its migrations, which included a spell of lying neglected in a field, a piece may have broken off the top. The object is now about seven feet tall. Running down one face of it is a worn Latin inscription in sixth-century lettering which says 'Drustanus lies here, the son of Cunomorus'. 'Drustanus' is another version of the extremely variable 'Tristan', and the stone is called the Tristan Stone. 'Cunomorus' is a Latin form of 'Kynvawr', the name of a king who ruled in Cornwall during the first half of the sixth century and was also active across the Channel in Brittany. There is good reason to think that Castle Dore was a residence of his.

He had dealings with an itinerant holy man, St Paul Aurelian. The author of this saint's 'life', many years afterwards, stated that Cunomorus was also called Mark. His full Latin style was Marcus Cunomorus. Evidently Mark and Tristan were fixed in this area by a belief that the prince on the monument was *the* Tristan and that 'Cunomorus' in the inscription was simply another name for the Mark of the story-tellers. Most scholars who have considered this belief think it mistaken, but some defend it. If the latter are right, the chief male characters existed and the tale may go back to actual happenings in Cornwall, though there is no doubt that it has ingredients from other parts of the British Isles. Marcus Cunomorus could have been an adventurer who started from Wales and attained power in the Dumnonian realm of the south-west, but left a reputation behind him that spread far afield with the wanderings of popular legend.

That is a viable guess, no more, and it still leaves a dangling awkwardness. If the inscription is correct, Tristan was Mark's son, not his nephew. And if so, Mark had a previous wife who was Tristan's mother, and Isolde was his second wife, Tristan's stepmother. Perfectly possible, but even more discreditable. Maybe some minstrel converted Tristan into a nephew for the lovers' benefit.

5. The Track of a Magician

DINAS EMRYS

WE HAVE STILL NOT PARTED COMPANY with Tintagel, not quite. Uther's entry, in his audacious disguise, opens up a major question. Merlin contrives it for him. Where does Merlin come from, and who is he? Geoffrey of Monmouth, who tells the tale, supplies the answer. He it is who brings Merlin on to the literary stage, not only in an earlier chapter of his *History*, but in a long narrative poem he wrote later.

Merlin's story begins in the time of Vortigern, the king who gives the Saxons their fatal footing in Britain. When they shook off his control and ravaged the country, Vortigern, Geoffrey tells us, fled to Wales and tried to build a fortress in Snowdonia. I mentioned that incident before, but not the outcome. The building materials kept vanishing. Vortigern's wizards told him that he must find a boy without a father, kill him, and sprinkle his blood on the foundations. In the town afterwards called Carmarthen a boy was discovered whose mother had been impregnated by a semi-spiritual being: in medieval language, an incubus. So her son at least had no human father and that was good enough. The son was Merlin.

When brought to the building site to be sacrificed, he outwitted the wizards by superior seership. He asked them what was below the ground, and they had no idea. He told Vortigern there was a subterranean pool, and there was. It had been swallowing up everything the workmen placed there. Then he invited them to say what was in the pool, and again they had no idea. He said it had two dragons in it. Vortigern had the pool drained and the dragons appeared, a red one and a white one, which fought each other. At first the white dragon had the best of it, but the red one recovered and drove the white back. Merlin interpreted the monsters as representing the Britons and Saxons (this, by the way, is the explanation of the Red Dragon of Wales). He foretold that Vortigern would be overthrown and slain, that Aurelius Ambrosius and Uther would follow him, and that a greater leader—that is, Arthur—would push the Saxons back. All came to pass as he predicted.

This scene raises several issues. For one thing, Merlin makes his début as a sort of juvenile prodigy. Afterwards he seems to mature fast, but he can hardly have been much past forty during the reign of Arthur. Who perpetrated our semi-comic image of him as an old man with a long white beard? I have a suspicion that it doesn't go back further than Tennyson.

Next, the place where the scene happens can be identified. It is Dinas Emrys, a hill-fort beside the valley of Nant Gwynant, a mile or so north-east of Beddgelert along the A498. Fragmentary remains of three lines of fortification surround an enclosure which is larger than Castle Dore's but not as large as Cadbury's. Excavation has disclosed a remarkable past. There was a Roman building, and near by there actually was a pool, an artificial one dug in the first century AD, though with no traces of dragons then or later. During the fifth century someone lived on the hill, who, to judge from the objects found, was a Christian and fairly affluent. As at Tintagel and other places, the story reflects remote historical facts, including details like the pool, however we may care to interpret them.

Local lore adds more about Merlin. He stayed on for a while after Vortigern left. When he himself left, he filled a golden cauldron with treasure and hid it in a cave, blocking the entrance with a stone and a heap of earth. The treasure is intended for one particular person, a youth with blue eyes and yellow hair. When he approaches, a bell will ring and the cave will unblock itself. Other treasure-seekers have been repulsed by storms and sinister omens.

'Dinas Emrys' means 'Fort of Ambrosius'. Geoffrey tells us that Merlin was 'also called Ambrosius'. He puts this in to resolve a difficulty. He is developing a much earlier account in the *Historia Brittonum* compiled (maybe) by Nennius, and there the young seer is called Ambrosius, not Merlin. 'Nennius' thinks he was the same person as the historical leader of that name, displaying paranormal gifts in his youth. Geoffrey implies that 'Nennius' got his Ambrosii mixed up, and considering how many things he does get mixed up, the implication is at least well invented. In Geoffrey's handling of the fifth-century characters, the leader Ambrosius comes through as Uther's elder brother, and the Ambrosius of the hill-fort, whoever he actually was, is Merlin under another name. On the one hand, this is all evidence for old traditions. On the other, it shows that they got distinctly confused.

So much for Dinas Emrys and the first scene of Merlin's public career. Before leaving, it is worth taking a glance along the valley below with its pleasant river, towards the lake Llyn Dinas, the Lake of the Fort. Close to it a warrior named Owein is said to have fought a giant. Taking cover in hollows

Nant Gwynant valley in North Wales, looking towards Dinas Emrys, the hill-fort where Merlin makes his first appearance in a confrontation with Vortigern. Below, a warrior named Owein fought a giant. Comparison of legends hints at a tradition making Owein a brother-in-law of Vortigern, so that the stories, far back, may be connected.

The pillar of Eliseg in Valle Crucis, near Llangollen. A memorial stone dating from the ninth century. Its original inscription, almost blotted out by a much later one, traces the royal line of Powys back to Vortigern and asserts that he married a daughter of the emperor Maximus.

Opposite above
Dunster Castle, Somerset. A much older fort, on or near the castle site, is named as a residence of Arthur in a story of the Welsh saint Carannog. The saint captures a giant serpent which Arthur has been pursuing without success.

Opposite below
Tintagel, Cornwall. On the headland stood the legendary castle of Gorlois, Duke of Cornwall, where King Uther reached Gorlois's wife Ygerna with Merlin's aid and begot Arthur. Remains of a real castle, at the landward end, are medieval, but archaeology has revealed the presence of an important settlement on the headland in the early post-Roman centuries.

Above
A valley in the region of southern Scotland once covered by the Forest of
Celidon or Caledonian Wood, where Merlin wandered distraught after the
battle at Arfderydd.

Opposite above
A view in the Isles of Scilly with the island Great Arthur in the distance. Some
of the Scillies were joined together in historical times. The sea's encroachment
here is part of the explanation for the legend of Lyonesse and its
disappearance.

Opposite below
St Michael's Mount, off the coast at Marazion in Cornwall. The water round
about covers a submerged forest where people used to live. As in the Isles of
Scilly, the Cornish tales of Lyonesse preserve traditions of the land's
inundation, though medieval flooding due to very high tides may have
contributed.

in the ground, they shot missiles at each other, either arrows or balls of steel. Both perished. The oddity is that in a roundabout way, the legend links up with Vortigern. Owein is made out to have been a son of Maximus, an emperor who was proclaimed in Britain in 383. His name is a Welsh form of Eugenius. Across the north of Wales is Llangollen (named, as you may recall, from St Collen, who tried to exorcize Glastonbury Tor), and close to it is Valle Crucis, the Valley of the Cross, where, on a mound, is a monument known as the Pillar of Eliseg. It has writing carved on its surface, but the original inscription, over a thousand years old, traced a Welsh royal pedigree back to Vortigern and said he married a daughter of Maximus. Geoffrey drops a circuitous hint at the same belief. Whatever its historical value, it would have made Maximus's reputed son Owein, the giant-fighter, a brother-in-law to Vortigern. Behind the Dinas Emrys tale there may be a lost Welsh dynastic saga telling why both Vortigern and Owein came to these parts.

Geoffrey credits Merlin with a series of cryptic prophecies about the future of Britain, uttered beside the pool, but after the climactic prediction of Vortigern's doom he leaves him for a while and passes to other characters. Merlin's second exploit is a surprising one, which takes him to Ireland and to Wiltshire.

STONEHENGE

Geoffrey relates how the royal brothers, Aurelius Ambrosius and Uther, deposed Vortigern as Merlin foretold. Aurelius became king, and one of his priorities, after containing the Saxons and repairing some of the damage they had done, was to raise a monument for 460 nobles whom the Saxon chieftain Hengist had massacred. They were buried in a mass grave near Amesbury. Uncertain what form the memorial should take, he sent for Merlin, who now had a reputation both for seership and, rather mysteriously, for skill with 'mechanical contrivances'. Aurelius hoped he would utter some more prophecies. Merlin refused to perform for the court's amusement, but offered a proposal for the memorial.

In Ireland, he said, there stood a circle of huge stones called the *Chorea Gigantum*, the Giants' Ring. Long ago giants had brought the stones from Africa. The Ring was used in religious rites, and the stones had healing pro-

Opposite above
Merlin's Hill near Carmarthen in Dyfed, south-west Wales, reputed birthplace of the enchanter. According to a local legend, the cave where he was imprisoned is in the lower part of this hill, and if you listen in the right place you can hear him groaning underground.

Opposite below
Bardsey Island off the north-west tip of Wales. Another Merlin legend says he is still living on this island in an invisible house of glass. In the house are various treasures including the true throne of Britain, on which Arthur will be enthroned when he returns.

perties. Water poured over them could cure the sick. The whole structure might be transplanted to Britain and set up around the grave.

Aurelius sent an expedition to Ireland headed by Uther. Merlin accompanied it. Irish warriors tried to defend the Ring, but the Britons drove them off. Uther's companions set to work with ladders and ropes, but failed to shift any of the stones. Merlin laughed, 'placed in position all the gear which he considered necessary', and dismantled the circle. The stones were loaded aboard ships and transported to Britain, then overland to the burial site, where Aurelius held a ceremony at Whitsun and Merlin reconstituted the circle . . . and that is how Stonehenge came to be on Salisbury Plain.

Merlin's technique is left vague. I'm not sure whether it is intended to be magical or simply ahead of his contemporaries. As for Geoffrey's giants, he mentions them earlier in the *History*. So far as they have any reality, they are the vanished megalith-building people who lived in the British Isles before the Celts, and are pictured as huge because of the difficulty of seeing how ordinary humans could have raised such colossal stones. In the case of Stonehenge, not only the size but the architectural design, especially the use of lintels or crosspieces, could have suggested the need for a wonder-worker like Merlin when the giants were extinct.

Stonehenge was not, of course, ferried bodily from Ireland in the fifth

century AD. It was built on its present site, in stages, thousands of years earlier. But the smaller 'bluestones' inside the major circle make the Merlin story look less purely fanciful. They are not local. Apparently they were quarried in the Prescelly Mountains in south-west Wales between Carn Meini and Foel Trigarn. If so, they would have been floated up the Bristol Channel on rafts, then doubtless up the Bristol Avon to a point demanding a minimum of overland haulage, so that Geoffrey's account of sea-borne stones from the west may have something in it, a glimmer of folk-memory. Some geologists have queried the need for such a far-away source, but Professor Colin Renfrew, who is generally held to know best, sticks to the Welsh origin.

What Geoffrey got hold of was perhaps a lost legend of a god or magician who built Stonehenge with stones from the west. Unaware of the monument's real age, or simply not considering it, he annexed the legend to Merlin. Had he any special reason for doing it, beyond a wish to make Merlin wonderful? Possibly he had. But let us follow his enchanter the rest of the way, and then ask again.

Of the Merlin of his *History* there is not much more to tell. Uther, impressed by the seer's powers, keeps him in his own entourage. Aurelius's reign is cut short. He dies at Winchester, poisoned by a Saxon with the connivance of a revengeful son of Vortigern. A portent appears in the sky, a brilliant star with a dragon. Rays of light stream from the dragon's mouth, one of them reaching out over Gaul. Merlin, who is with Uther's army on another campaign, interprets the apparition. Aurelius is dead, the star and dragon symbolize Uther who succeeds him, and the ray stretching over Gaul is Uther's son: a second foreshadowing of Arthur, who will lead the Britons across the Channel.

Uther has two golden replicas of the dragon made, one for Winchester Cathedral, the other as a sort of mascot to carry with him. The portent is the reason for his being called Pendragon himself. Geoffrey says it means 'dragon's head', actually it means 'head dragon', the word 'dragon' being used in Welsh for a military leader. Not long after Uther's accession he holds that Easter banquet attended by Gorlois and Ygerna, with the famous consequence at Tintagel. In arranging the begetting of Uther's prophesied son, Merlin is definitely a worker of magic.

THE NORTH

Surprisingly again, in view of what Malory, Tennyson, T. H. White and film-makers would lead us to expect, Geoffrey is almost silent about the role of

Opposite
Stonehenge, on Salisbury Plain. Many of the stones have gone, but enough are still there to show the pattern of this unique monument. Geoffrey of Monmouth says it formerly stood in Ireland, and was brought to Britain through Merlin's arts. Actually it is far earlier, though some of the smaller stones, visible inside the main circle, do seem to have been brought from a long way off.

Drumelzier in Tweeddale, where the burn Pausayl runs into the Tweed. In the northern legend of Merlin his grave is near here, perhaps at a place where the burn formed another confluence during a spate in 1603, fulfilling (it is said) a prophecy about the union of the crowns of Scotland and England.

Merlin at the court of Arthur himself. For practical purposes the Tintagel affair is his last appearance. Some years after the *History*, however, Geoffrey wrote a *Life of Merlin* in Latin verse. Its title, like the title of the *History*, is misleading, though in a different way. The poem is confined to events after Arthur's passing. In composing it, Geoffrey fudged dates and details to make Merlin's later life fit on to what he had said in the *History*. He had to do this because he was now working with other traditions, from Cumbria and Scotland, and these in fact did *not* fit.

After Arthur's departure, it seems, Merlin enjoyed fame and influence. Then a catastrophe disrupted his life and rekindled his prophetic gifts in a wilder, stranger form. He was involved in a tragic battle among the Britons themselves, near what is now the Scottish border. It was a clash remembered in Wales as 'futile' because it was fought over a lark's nest. That phrase is a bitter joke. The theme of dispute was a stronghold on the north side of the Solway Firth, Caerlaverock, the Fort of the Lark. One combatant was a Cumbrian chief, Gwenddolau, whose own stronghold was Caer Gwenddolau, a name that has become Carwinley. Carwinley today is a quiet spot among woods and low hills, but traces of fortifications can be discerned nearer Liddel Water. The battle was fought not far away, at Arfderydd. That name too survives in the border parish of Arthuret (no connection with Arthur). Some of Gwenddolau's enemies were his own relatives, so that the battle had the peculiar horror of civil warfare. The principal leader on the opposing side was Rhydderch, who ruled Strathclyde, then a British kingdom covering much of southern Scotland with its capital at Dumbarton, the 'Fort of the Britons'.

Merlin, appalled at the carnage and oppressed with guilt for his own share in it, was driven out of his mind. He wandered northwards into the Forest of Celidon, or Caledonian Wood, which covered Dumfries and Selkirk and the head-waters of the Clyde and Tweed. There he lived as a hermit, suffering and lamenting. But he met Rhydderch and others of the northern nobility, and spoke bizarre prophecies. As his sanity returned he also met the bard Taliesin, who gave him details of Arthur's voyage to Avalon. Merlin's sister Ganieda befriended him. They had an observatory built to study the heavens, and she grew to share his prophetic powers.

The end remains obscure, but, as at Dinas Emrys, older legends which Geoffrey is using and manipulating can still be traced behind his text. They told how the seer prophesied three different deaths for himself, a seeming absurdity that was thought to discredit him. But when he exposed the infidelity of a king's wife, she persuaded her husband's shepherds to kill him, and they gave him a beating and threw him into the Tweed, where his body was pierced by a stake, so that he did die from three causes—by blows, by impalement and by drowning. The details vary in different versions. In another he falls from a cliff, gets his feet caught, and hangs head-down in the water, so that he dies by falling, hanging, and—again—drowning.

His grave is at Drumelzier in Tweeddale. The hills open out around the tiny village, forming a flat valley floor with the Tweed flowing along it. A burn, the Pausayl (Willow), runs down through trees beside a bluff with a church on it. Coming out into the open, the Pausayl curves around the base of the bluff and goes on through fields to join the Tweed. The grave's location is uncertain. It may be near the foot of the bluff. But if you follow a track, you come to a stone that may mark the spot. A now-vanished cairn close to the river is mentioned in a couplet attributed to the Scots poet Thomas the Rhymer, a seer himself:

> When Tweed and Pausayl meet at Merlin's grave,
> Scotland and England shall one monarch have.

During a spate in 1603 the Pausayl changed its course and met the Tweed near the cairn. In the same year James VI of Scotland became James I of England also, and the two kingdoms, for the first time, had one monarch. So perhaps Merlin was under the cairn. His name is preserved in Merlindale, across the bridge over the Tweed.

CARMARTHEN

You may protest that this doesn't sound like the Merlin you know. The truth is that Geoffrey was trying to combine traditions of two seers more than a hundred years apart, one in Wales and one in the north, and the result was naturally confusing and didn't, in the end, stand up, though even the attempt raises fascinating and tantalizing questions.

He got the actual name from Welsh sources that refer to the second of the two, the northerner. Strictly speaking it is 'Myrddin'. When Geoffrey adapted it he put an L instead of a D because he had to reckon with Norman-French readers for whom 'Merdin' would suggest *merde*, a dirty word. By collating Welsh and Scottish records we can put together something about the northern man. In fact, owing to Geoffrey's obfuscation, a proper understanding of parts of his poem depends on consulting them. The battle at Arfderydd which drove the northerner out of his mind was fought late in the sixth century. While the prophetic lunacy sounds fabulous, there is a hint at some sort of reality in references to him under another name, Lailoken.

Geoffrey's identification of him with the lad who confronted Vortigern long before looks like a sheer muddle. Yet if we ask where the style 'Myrddin' came from, curious considerations arise. It is connected with Carmarthen. 'Carmarthen' in Welsh is Myrddin Town, supposedly named after the seer because he was born there. Actually it's the other way round. 'Myrddin' is derived from the town's old name, *Moridunum* as the Romans made it, and the seer is, so to speak, a Myrddin-man.

Carmarthen has a hill and other neighbourhood features echoing the leg-

Near Carmarthen, Dyfed. Woods on Bryn Myrddin, Merlin's Hill. 'Myrddin' is his name in Welsh, and is derived from the old form of the name of Carmarthen. The relation between the seer's name and the town's is open to conjecture.

ends. Near the city centre an ancient tree used to stand, Myrddin's Tree or Priory Oak. According to a popular rhyme:

> When Myrddin's Tree shall tumble down,
> Then shall fall Carmarthen town.

Civic authorities tried to avert that disaster by bracing the tree with iron supports and putting a railing round it, but it has now been removed, and all you can see is a specimen of its wood in the town museum.

The fact that both the Merlins or Myrddins have other names of their own—Ambrosius, Lailoken—suggests a faint possibility that Geoffrey was not a complete muddler here; and that there was a real bond between the two because, owing to some myth attached to Carmarthen, 'Myrddin' was a sobri-

Merlin's Rock, Mousehole. One of several places in Cornwall where Merlin's fame as a prophet survives. He is reputed to have uttered this couplet: 'There shall land on the Rock of Merlin, Those who shall burn Paul, Penzance and Newlyn.' While he would not have spoken English, there is a slightly more plausible Cornish version. The couplet refers to a Spanish raid in 1595, but may have been made up after the event.

quet meaning an inspired person or prophet and did apply to both. In one or two early Welsh texts, 'Myrddin' sounds like a spirit of inspiration rather than an individual. In Geoffrey's *History* itself Merlin twice mentions his controlling spirit. Could it be that both the seers counted as Myrddin-men or Myrddins, and Geoffrey, vaguely aware of this but lacking the key, tried to make out that they were the same person? A much later Welsh author, Elis Gruffudd, conscious that they lived more than a century apart yet sensing that they were linked, tried to explain their identity by reincarnation, so that one of the Merlins *was* the other carrying on in a new life.

Ingenious. But let's indulge a fancy. Let's suppose that long before Christianity there was a god in Britain something like the Greek Apollo, a god of inspiration. He had an oracle near the town eventually called Carmarthen, Myrddin Town, like Apollo's oracle at Delphi. Look at the map: Stonehenge's bluestones were quarried in the Prescelly Mountains less than twenty miles away. Let fancy continue. Through the magic stones from his own territory, transported to Salisbury Plain, the god gave sacred power to Stonehenge, so

Ruins of old Dynevor Castle, up the Tywi from Carmarthen. Edmund Spenser, in *The Faerie Queene*, says Merlin used to commune with spirits in a cave in the wooded hillside.

that Stonehenge was his creation. Folk-memories of the myth lingered on. Inspired prophets came to be known from the oracular place as Myrddin-men, perhaps Myrddin-women too. Geoffrey knew traditions of three of these Myrddins—the divine maker of Stonehenge, retroactively the Myrddin-god; a fifth-century inspired prophet; and a sixth-century inspired prophet—and he rolled them all together into a single figure, who set up Stonehenge, confronted Vortigern, and wandered in the northern wilds.

Edmund Spenser, in his *Faerie Queene*, has a very odd passage. He speaks of a cave in the grounds of Dynevor Castle, on Carmarthen's river Tywi but quite a long way farther up it:

> There the wise Merlin whilom wont (they say)
> To make his wonne [dwelling] low underneath the ground,
> In a deep delve, far from the view of day,
> That of no living wight he might be found,
> When he so counselled with his sprites encompassed round.
>
> And if thou ever happen that same way
> To travel, go to see that dreadful place:
> It is an hideous hollow cave (they say)
> Under a rock that lies a little space
> From the swift Barry, tumbling down apace,
> Amongst the woody hills of Dynevowre;
> But dare thou not, I charge, in any case,
> To enter into that same baleful bower,
> For fear the cruel fiends should thee unwares devour.

Spenser adds that if you listen from outside, you can still hear disturbing noises from under the rock. He weakens the description slightly by getting the name of the river wrong. But the passage does have rather an air of folk-reminiscence of a heathen place, an oracular cavern like the ones in which Apollo and other beings spoke to intimidated and awestruck Greeks. Certainly Spenser couldn't have got it from the familiar Merlin literature.

AT THE KING'S COURT

As I said, Geoffrey's composite character turned out not to be viable. The romancers who followed knew which portion of Merlin's life they cared about. It was the portion that lay in the fifth century. They took little interest in the northern wanderings, even rejecting them as part of the story, though a few hints from them survived. That rejection persisted into modern times. T. H. White's erudite wizard in *The Once and Future King* is wholly contemporary with Uther and Arthur. As far as I know, the only treatment of the Arthurian Legend that includes Merlin's post-Arthur phase is the play *The Island of the Mighty*, by John Arden and Margaretta d'Arcy.

Romancers saw the potentialities of the fifth-century part, and saw the amazing gap Geoffrey had left. He had said virtually nothing of the enchanter during Arthur's reign. They moved in gladly to fill the vacuum, making Merlin not only foretell Arthur and mastermind his birth, but attend him as he attended Uther, in the role of counsellor and magical helper. The result was a great literary creation, and a remarkable one. It was as if Merlin had indeed been latently a god all along, blossoming out in romance as divine once again, the sponsor of Britain's Golden Age.

The Merlin of romance brings about Arthur's birth, not merely to oblige Uther, but to produce a kind of Messiah. He takes the child away, to be fostered in obscure safety till his hour comes. He contrives the Sword-in-the-Stone test to prove Arthur's title. He helps the King in his early struggles, giving him prophetic glimpses of the way things will go, and sometimes warning him. He arranges for Arthur to get the sword Excalibur from the Lady of the Lake. He designs the Round Table which, in due course, becomes the mystical focus of the knighthood. He even prepares the way for the Grail Quest.

This Merlin departs long before the decline sets in. He falls victim to a woman, foreseeing his doom, but knowing how it must be. Obsessed with desire for the lake-damsel Nimue or Viviane (her name varies), he travels with her, revealing various magical secrets, till she becomes tired of him and uses a spell to imprison him in a cave or tomb or invisible enclosure (that too varies). No more is said of him. If he survived, and had his northern adventures in a mysteriously prolonged old age, and died and was buried, he must have escaped sooner or later. But we are never told.

Maybe this is an anti-feminist libel. The Welsh have a legend making Merlin an immortal like Arthur. He is on Bardsey Island off the north-western tip of Wales. The island has remains of an ancient monastery, and was once a place of pilgrimage. Twenty thousand monks are alleged to be buried there, an exaggeration, and ghosts in cowls pace along the beach when shipwrecks are imminent.

Merlin is on Bardsey by his own wish, not because his inamorata trapped him. If she was involved, it was surely a work of benign enchantment by consenting adults. Some say he is asleep, like Arthur in his cave, but he may be awake and active still. His home is an invisible house of glass, and he has nine companions with him. In the house are the Thirteen Treasures of Britain, ancient magical objects concealed from the Saxons and other foreigners. They include a cloak of invisibility, a chariot that takes you instantly wherever you want, a chess set that plays by itself, and a sword that bursts into flames when drawn. Besides these anticipations of chess computers and the *Star Wars* laser weapon, Merlin has the true royal throne of Britain. When Arthur returns, his faithful magician will bring it out and enthrone him.

6. The King Himself

THE CAMPAIGNS

BUT WHAT ABOUT ARTHUR'S FIRST ENTHRONEMENT? Despite all the romantic flowering, it is not easy to give his reign geographical substance. Of the places where local legend has taken root, more are due to popular tales and poems—to saga-type matter, largely unwritten, largely lost—than to the courtly literature of the Middle Ages. However familiar the romance-image of 'King Arthur and the Knights of the Round Table', it has not stamped itself widely on the map. We have to grope about behind it.

As we noted already, the oldest consecutive account of Arthur by name, in the ninth-century *Historia Brittonum* of Nennius (or whoever), lists twelve battles which he won as the Britons' war-leader against the Anglo-Saxons and probably Pictish allies of theirs. The place-names are given in Welsh forms, and some of them have been blotted out by English-speaking supplanters, so that we cannot be sure what places are meant. Others can be identified. Arthur is stated to have fought battles on a river Glein, and in a region called Linnuis. Glein is probably the Lincolnshire Glen, and Linnuis is probably Lindsey, the central and northern portion of the same county. Angles were settled thereabouts before the middle of the fifth century. Two other battles were fought in the Forest of Celidon, where Merlin afterwards wandered, and in the City of the Legion, which here means Chester. Both of these would fit in with an early date, as battles in Lincolnshire would. In fact, they almost imply it. The northern forest suggests Picts, who were involved in the barbarian outbreak

Opposite
Badbury Rings, Dorset. A triple-ramparted hill-fort in level country, proposed as Mount Badon, the scene of a British victory over the Saxons often credited to Arthur.

of the mid-fifth century, but not—so far as we know—later, while Chester is so far west that Arthur could only have fought there during the same chaotic period, when barbarians raided at will across the country.

On the other hand, the same list credits Arthur with the victory of Mount Badon, which gave a temporary check to Saxon encroachment. Badon seems to have been fought somewhere about 500, and an Arthur active in 450–60 is unlikely to have been the war-leader so long after. If he was indeed the same person as Riothamus, who fades from view in 470, it seems out of the question. Since 'Nennius' says he killed 960 men single-handed in the battle, his Badon connection has a distinctly legendary look. The Welsh do not seem to have attached much importance to it, and their early vernacular tradition never mentions Badon.

Still, Badon is often linked with Arthur's name. Maybe the Arthur of legend is a composite like Geoffrey's Merlin, combining an earlier and a later leader. Another possibility follows from a Welsh poem that speaks of a force called 'Arthur's men' fighting in his absence and perhaps after his death. Battles in which 'Arthur's men' played a leading role could have come to be remembered inaccurately as battles where he led in person.

Anyhow, where was Mount Badon? Geoffrey displaces the victory in time and sets it on one of the hills overlooking Bath, where the Roman baths are

called *balnea Badonis* in a Latin text. Some historians believe he was right. The hill-fort Little Solsbury, north-east of the city, would be a good candidate, though it has no signs of fifth-century reoccupation. Another candidate is Badbury Rings, a hill-fort in Dorset, near Wimborne. This has a well-preserved triple rampart carved out of chalky soil. In contrast with Cadbury, the fortifications are largely in the open, whereas the enclosure is wooded. Until recently this was one of the few English breeding-places of ravens, the large sort who live in the Tower of London. The objection to Badbury Rings is its distance from the main areas of Saxon settlement. It is hard to see how a battle there could have involved enough numbers to have any decisive result.

A third possibility—maybe the best, at present—is Liddington Castle, a hill-fort south of Swindon, which has a village of Badbury near its foot and used to be known as Badbury Castle. It rises nine hundred feet above sea-level, commanding a wide expanse of country, including a gap in the hills through which an enemy trying to reach the West Country might have marched. A trial excavation in 1976 showed that the top rampart was refurbished in the fifth century, though nothing like the Cadbury refortification was attempted, and there were no traces of long-term settlement. Rosemary Sutcliff located Badon here in her novel *Sword at Sunset*.

Even without Badon, the list spreads Arthur's campaigning widely. By the time it was put together he was manifestly thought of as a national rather than a local hero, a high king or commander-in-chief, and two of the Welsh saints' 'lives' make him explicitly king of Britain, if with a certain ambiguity as to what the title amounted to. His kingship in medieval literature is at least grounded on earlier ideas of him.

THE COURT

While Arthur's rise in romance takes various forms, everybody accepts, as 'Nennius' does, that he had a great deal of fighting to do—against barbarians, or Britons who contested his right, or both. Everybody accepts also that he won, and gave Britain a spell of peace. It is during this peace that most of the adventures and quests of his knights are portrayed as taking place.

The Welsh tale *Culhwch and Olwen* introduces him at home with a catalogue of 200-odd followers. Some of them are warriors known to romance also, such as Kay and Bedivere. Others are fairy-tale characters who can run along tree-tops, hear ants in the ground fifty miles off, and drink the sea dry till ships lie stranded. *Culhwch and Olwen* is marvellous fun, full of ferocity and comedy, giants and monsters. As we might expect, however, it is Geoffrey once again who provides the first real picture of Arthur's court, the first real foreshadowing of Camelot.

He tells how, after organizing his conquests in Gaul, Arthur held a magnificent Whitsun ceremony at Caerleon upon Usk, in south-east Wales. Caerleon was the site of the Roman legionary fortress Isca Silurum. Ruined walls still show the layout of its buildings, and near by is an amphitheatre, the finest specimen in Britain, uncovered by excavation. In the twelfth century there were remains of baths, vaults, central-heating systems. Nothing, however, indicates any post-Roman use, and Geoffrey doubtless picked the place because it was close to his home town and had plainly been a centre of population grand enough to suit King Arthur. He improved it, inventing two famous churches, and a college with two hundred scholars, whose skills included astrological forecasting, Merlin having perhaps declined to co-operate.

Arthur's Whitsun ceremony is a plenary court with a public crown-wearing, attended by his sub-kings, nobles and higher ecclesiastics. This has nothing to do with history, it is an updating exercise modelled on the ritual of Norman kingship. Geoffrey gives a tremendous list of those in attendance. Among them are Auguselus, king of Scotland; Cadwallo, king of North

Opposite
Caerleon, Gwent. The amphitheatre in what was once an important Roman centre. Geoffrey of Monmouth, whose home town was not very far away, imagines Arthur holding court here and gives a description that supplies many hints for the Camelot of romance.

Wales; and Cador, the Cornish ruler whom we have met before. There are three archbishops, of London, York and Caerleon itself, the last being Dubricius, who is primate of Arthur's kingdom and has a gift of healing. Overseas monarchs subject to Arthur include the kings of Ireland, Iceland and Norway. Geoffrey enlarges the catalogue by copying names from old Welsh genealogies, irrespective of the dates of the persons concerned. Among the characters are some who are, or may have been, real people, more or less in Arthur's time. The most important are Dubricius, who is the Welsh saint Dyfrig; Loth, Gawain's father, who may conceivably be Leudonus, a king of Lothian in Scotland; and Cador, Kay and Bedivere, more properly Cadwy, Cai and Bedwyr. Kay has the role he keeps in romance, as Arthur's seneschal or manager of the royal household.

After the King and Queen have been duly enthroned and crowned, celebrations are held.

> By this time (says Geoffrey) Britain had reached such a standard of sophistication that it excelled all other kingdoms in its general affluence, the richness of its decorations, and the courteous behaviour of its inhabitants. Every knight in the country who was in any way famed for his bravery wore livery and arms showing his own distinctive colour; and women of fashion often displayed the same colours. They scorned to give their love to any man who had not proved himself three times in battle. In this way the womenfolk became chaste and more virtuous and for their love the knights were ever more daring.

At Caerleon the knights competed in tournaments, while other ranks engaged in archery, javelin-throwing, and sedentary games such as dice. The festivities went on for four days. Arthur awarded lavish prizes to the winners in each class.

The romancers after Geoffrey describe similar occasions. In their work, Caerleon remains an Arthurian centre. But Carlisle too is important. So is Camelot. The splendid Camelot of romance is not, of course, Cadbury Castle, and as I remarked before, there is no point in looking for it anywhere else. The hints at its whereabouts are hazy and inconsistent. Malory is exceptional in making it out to be Winchester, which sometimes functioned as England's capital before the pre-eminence of London. Here, however, he goes astray, because Camelot is not the national capital but the personal headquarters of Arthur, and Malory's own editor Caxton disagrees with him.

A central feature of Camelot is the Round Table. Geoffrey speaks of an

Opposite
The King's Knot below Stirling Castle in Scotland. Most of it was originally a
royal garden laid out in the seventeenth century, but the central mound is
called the Round Table and may be older. There are medieval references to a
'Tabyll Round' at Stirling.

Arthurian order of knights, enrolling men of note from all countries, but he never mentions a special piece of furniture. It may have come into the legend by way of Brittany. At first Arthur is said to have had the Table made for a practical reason. He wanted to prevent quarrels over precedence, since, at a long table, the end nearer the King would be too obviously the more honourable. Later the Round Table becomes symbolic. Designed by Merlin, it belongs first to Uther, then passes to Guinevere's father Leodegan, then to Arthur with Guinevere as her dowry. It is meant to recall two previous tables, that of the Last Supper, and another on which the Grail was placed, so that it links the earthly with the spiritual. Also its shape is an image of the round world and heavens. The difficulty is always that, on the face of it, no table could have been big enough to seat as many knights as Arthur is stated to have had—140 or 150 or even 250. Some medieval artists solve the problem after a fashion by making the Table a ring instead of a disc, with gaps for servitors to pass through.

Several earthworks and other formations have been dubbed 'the Round Table'. The name was given to the Roman amphitheatre at Caerleon before its unveiling by excavation. Covered with earth it was an enormous oval mound, sixteen feet high, with a central depression. The knights would have sat round

it facing inwards, as the Roman spectators did. Mayburgh, near Penrith in Cumbria, has another Round Table, a great heaped up platform surrounded by a ditch, with a bank outside the ditch, broken at two places to make entrances. This may be four thousand years old. Its purpose is unknown.

A third case, in Scotland, is more interesting. The chronicler William of Worcester, writing in 1478, informs his readers that King Arthur kept the Round Table at Stirling Castle. The Scottish poet Sir David Lindsay mentions Stirling's 'Chapell-royall, park, and Tabyll Round'. It may have been a raised platform of earth which is still there, incorporated into the King's Knot. The King's Knot, an arrangement of embankments and paths, originated in 1627 as a royal garden. As a garden it is long since defunct, but the layout is still excellently defined, as you can see from the castle walls. The Round Table is a mound at the centre, forty-odd feet across.

If this is medieval, or is a modification of a mound that was, it could have been a centre-piece for entertainments of a type called Round Tables, which were popular with royalty and nobility. Participants dressed up as Arthurian characters, banqueted and jousted. Several English kings held Round Tables, Edward I, for instance. I am not sure about Scottish ones. Arthur, who was alleged to have conquered the Scots, was apt to be viewed ambiguously north of the Border. Still, William of Worcester does indicate some legend of him at Stirling that might have inspired events of this sort.

In England they may account for a famous pseudo-Arthurian relic, the oaken Round Table hanging up in the hall of Winchester Castle. This is a table-top only, because the twelve legs that formerly fitted into it are all gone. It is eighteen feet across and was made in the thirteenth or fourteenth century, possibly for one of Edward I's Arthurian festivals. By Malory's time, to judge from the introduction with which Caxton prefaced his book, its origin was forgotten and it was assumed to be the real thing. In 1522 it was painted in segments, with places for the King and twenty-four rather crowded knights. Since then the design has been repainted but not changed. The segmented Table looks rather like a colossal dartboard.

ARTHURIAN CHARACTERS

For Geoffrey of Monmouth, as long as Arthur is on the stage at all he is central. For the romancers—especially the ones writing in French, who did most to create the developed Legend—this is not usually so. Interest shifts to the exploits and amours of his knights, and the King tends to be little more

Opposite
The Round Table in Winchester Castle Hall, actually a table-top only, since the legs are lost. It may have been made for an Arthurian festival of a kind that was staged by kings and nobles during the Middle Ages. The design was painted on it in 1522 for the youthful Henry VIII, who was himself the model for the King.
(Michael Holford Library)

Bamburgh Castle, Northumberland. Speaking of Lancelot's Joyous Gard, Malory says it may have been either here or at Alnwick. The Bamburgh site has a longer history and is a more likely source for any tradition there may have been.

than a magnificent chairman, whose court is chiefly a starting-point for adventures. He remains a noble figure. There is less about war, more about his concern for justice and chivalry. He is wise and kind, and can take firm action when action is called for, but he becomes more of a symbol of majesty and Christian ideals, less of a person. This is not invariably so. A few romances present him as weak, jealous and worse. But his dignity survives as a rule, even when his wife is unfaithful.

With the shift of interest to his companions, there is a shift away from even tenuous fact, and therefore from geography. Some of the continental romancers show a vague knowledge of Britain, but don't seem to care much, and even English ones seldom supply convincing locations.

Lancelot, who is a latecomer popularized by the French, has a northern castle called Joyous Gard. At first this is merely north of the Humber, apparently close to it, but Malory corrects that impression and pins it down... almost. 'Some men say it was Alnwick and some men say it was Bamburgh.' Bamburgh, on the coast of Northumberland, was the capital of the ancient Northumbrian kingdom. The present castle is not old as castles go; but the site was fortified by the Angles, and before they took over it had a British fort on it, Din Guayrdi. This name, which is preserved in Welsh matter, may have been noticed because it was like the French *garde* meaning 'protection' or 'defence', and converted into a name for the stronghold of Lancelot.

At least we have a slender historical excuse for picturing an Arthurian noble at Bamburgh, looking out over the sea to the Farne Islands. Even apart from Lancelot the place has a colourful folklore, including tales of the wonder-working St Aidan, and a princess transformed into a dragon by her wicked stepmother, who, very properly foiled, now lives below the castle in the form of a toad. Lancelot, we are told, captured the original castle when it was under an evil enchantment and called Dolorous Gard. Inside he found a tomb with his own name on it, and realized that this was his destined home and burial place. He renamed it Joyous Gard. Arthur and Guinevere came to it as his guests, and so did Tristan and Isolde. When his love-affair with the Queen was brought into the open, Arthur counted her infidelity as treason and she was condemned to be burnt to death at Carlisle. Lancelot rescued her from the stake and brought her to Joyous Gard. Arthur besieged it and Lancelot restored her, on condition that her life should be spared. Long after, when the King and Queen were gone and he died as a hermit near Glastonbury, his body was taken to Joyous Gard and buried in the long-prepared tomb.

Lancelot is known as 'Lancelot of the Lake' because he was taken away from his parents as a child and brought up by the Lady of the Lake. That phrase stands for an official position rather than an individual. The Ladies of the Lake reigned in succession, enchantresses heading a bevy of lake-damsels, among them the one who led Merlin to disaster. The background is pagan, and the Ladies may have been Celtic priestesses. Their Lake is 'a fair water and broad' but unidentified. My own favourite guess is that the original was Derwent Water in the Lake District. 'Derwent' is derived from a Celtic word for an oak-tree, and so is 'Druid'. Perhaps Derwent Water was named for the sacred oak-grove of a Druidess, the original Lady. And once again, I have a feeling that Guinevere belongs in the north, and that the tragedy of her amour may go back to some Celtic queen's love for a fellow-northerner, though it must be acknowledged that Lancelot is given a French birthplace, wherever he goes later.

Another conspicuous figure at the Round Table is Arthur's nephew Gawain. Whereas Lancelot is not born in the north, but makes a home there, Gawain is northern-born—in Scotland—but non-resident. Continental romancers put him in a poor light, and so does Malory, with the highly moral Tennyson following. On the other hand, several English stories make him the finest in all the company. He is the hero of the poetic tale of the Green Knight, who appears at Camelot during Christmas festivities and challenges any of Arthur's men to strike a blow at him, on the understanding that he can return the blow in a year's time. Gawain cuts the Green Knight's head off, assuming that the contract for the return blow will lapse. Disconcertingly, however, the Green Knight picks up his head and goes away none the worse. How Gawain keeps the tryst and comes through intact is the theme of this brilliant, anonymous fairy-tale. In his search for the Green Knight's home he goes to Wirral Forest, clearly Wirral in Cheshire, a royal forest in medieval times. But when the poet depicts this innocuous peninsula as a wilderness infested with wolves, bears, trolls, ogres and dragons, he does seem to be going a little far.

Another of Gawain's experiences is set in and near Carlisle, a town that figures in several Arthurian tales, probably because it survived longer than most into the post-Roman period, and may have been a base for resistance to the northern Angles. Near Carlisle, Arthur was taken prisoner by a sinister knight named Gromersomer, who let him go on condition that he would return on a set date (the same kind of requirement that the Green Knight imposed) with the answer to the question 'What do women most desire?' After much inconclusive inquiry, aided by Gawain, the King met a repulsive hag who gave him the answer—that women most desire to have their own way—and asked, as her reward, that Gawain should marry her. Always loyal to his liege, the knight consented. After their wedding she explained that she was under a spell and could be ugly by day and beautiful by night, or vice versa. Her husband must make a choice. Gawain chivalrously chose to let her decide for herself, and kissed her. The spell was broken and she became beautiful all the time.

Carlisle is also the scene of a clash which is a main cause of the Round Table's dissolution. When Guinevere is brought there to be burnt at the stake, and Lancelot saves her, he and his followers fight their way through a party of

Derwent Water, near Keswick in Cumbria. The name is derived partly from a Celtic British word for an oak and is thus related to 'Druid', which seems to mean an 'oak-knower', referring to a lore of trees. Derwent Water could have had a pagan sanctuary such as is dimly recalled in tales of the Lady of the Lake.

Coastline around St Govan's Head at the southern tip of Pembroke. William of Malmesbury says Gawain's grave was found somewhere in this part of Wales, though perhaps not very near here. But a legend claims that 'Govan' is a corruption of 'Gawain', in which case the notion of a separate St Govan must be due to a misunderstanding.

knights faithful to the King. Two of Gawain's brothers are killed and he becomes Lancelot's implacable enemy. They meet in combat several times, and Lancelot gives Gawain a wound which is not fatal at once, but eventually causes his death at Dover. Caxton, in his preface to Malory, speaks of Gawain's skull being kept at Dover Castle.

Older versions of Gawain's end place it in Wales. His grave is said to have been found on the Pembrokeshire coast in the reign of William the Conqueror. According to local legend he was interred or reinterred in St Govan's Chapel just west of St Govan's Head, the most southerly point on the coast near Pembroke. On this showing 'Govan' is a corruption of 'Gawain'. The chapel is in a break in the cliffs with steps descending from above and continuing downwards to the foot. Reputedly the steps cannot be counted, because you will always make it a different number when you go down from the number you make it when you go up. The chapel is medieval, but incorporates what may be remnants of an earlier hermitage, including an altar that is supposed to have the knight's tomb under it. This may all be a misunderstanding, and St Govan may have been a real and different person, a Welsh hermit. While nothing factual is known about him, there are legends of miracles. The chapel wall has a cleft in it where Govan (or Gawain?) hid when

Opposite
St Govan's Chapel. Interior. The final resting-place of the bones of Gawain—if
he is the real 'Govan'—is supposed to be under an altar on the right.

Above
The Giant's Grave in a churchyard at Penrith, Cumbria. Fifteen feet long, it is
alleged to be the grave of Owain, a sixth-century northern prince who
becomes, in medieval romance, the son of Morgan le Fay. In reality this is a
composite structure, made by grouping several old monuments.

pursued by enemies. The rock closed to hide him and opened again when they went away. If you stand in the cleft facing the wall, and make a wish, it will be granted so long as you don't change your mind before turning round.

Apart from the few like Tristan already discussed, not much can be done to locate other Arthurian characters in any but the cloudiest manner. Galahad's pursuit of the Grail takes him through no known territory. What about the enchantress Morgan le Fay? She is heard of first as a benign healer, but later she shows hostility to Arthur's people, and is behind the ordeals Gawain suffers in his Green Knight adventures. She is sometimes associated with a castle in Edinburgh mentioned by Geoffrey, but it is not clear why. So far as she has a deep-rooted traditional role, it is as the Lady of Avalon, which places her at Glastonbury—doubtless among the pre-Christian mysteries of the Tor—if it places her anywhere.

Morgan has a son Owain or Owein who is commemorated, if that is the right word, by one of the most bizarre monuments in England. Owain, who becomes Yvain in the hands of the French, is a respected member of the Round Table and has a story or two to himself. In his origins he is a real person, a northern prince who fought bravely against the Angles, and was extolled in poems by the bard Taliesin. At Penrith in Cumbria, in St Andrew's churchyard, is the Giant's Grave, supposedly his though it has no name on it. Two tapering stone pillars, which were once crosses, stand fifteen feet apart. In the space between are four carved 'hog-back' stones, half-circular in shape, resting on their straight edges. The arrangement gives the impression of a grave with a huge occupant, and legend asserts that in the reign of Elizabeth I his bones were dug up. The truth is that the Giant's Grave was formed by putting six tenth-century monuments together. If you care to believe that Owain lies buried here, so be it, but there is no reason to think that he stretched from pillar to pillar.

THE DOWNFALL

Arthur's end is cryptic. It is dominated by the theme of a tragic battle, Briton against Briton, which very likely happened, yet has a fundamental elusiveness that puts the battle of Badon in the shade.

Geoffrey first considers the King's departure when he is looking ahead in his account of Merlin prophesying before Vortigern. Merlin foretells the yet-unborn Arthur as 'the Boar of Cornwall' whose deeds will be 'as meat and drink to those who tell tales'. Arthur's triumphs will be strangely cut short.

> The Boar . . . shall lord it over the forests of Gaul.
> The House of Romulus shall dread the Boar's savagery
> and the end of the Boar will be shrouded in mystery.

At this point in his work, Geoffrey seems to have pictured Arthur as disap-

A sweep of country in southern Scotland, once part of the Forest of Celidon or Caledonian Wood, where Arthur is said to have fought one of his twelve battles. The far-flung spread of these battles implies a belief, at least by the ninth century, that he was a major national leader.

Bamburgh Castle on the coast of Northumberland. Malory says this may have been Sir Lancelot's stronghold Joyous Gard. The present castle is much later, but there was a British fort, probably early enough, which the northern Angles took over and made their capital.

The neighbourhood of Snowdon, the highest mountain in Wales, scene of a Welsh story of Arthur's last battle – one of several stories inspired by the vagueness of its location.

pearing from view during Roman involvements on the continent, hence, before the Empire's demise in the West—on the conventional reading, before the removal of the last western emperor in 476. This is in keeping with my belief that Arthur is based partly at least on Riothamus, who did campaign in Gaul, and does vanish from the historical record in Burgundy, in or about 470.

But as Geoffrey pushed ahead with the *History*, he evidently realized that the Welsh had their own version of Arthur's end. They claimed that he fell in the 'strife of Camlann' fighting another Briton, Medraut. According to a curt, unembroidered entry in the tenth-century *Annales Cambriae* or Annals of Wales, Camlann occurred in 539. This is one of two *Annales* allusions to Arthur which are in conflict not only with Geoffrey but with other early testimony. Yet they cannot simply be brushed aside. If Arthur is a blend of two heroes, or even more, perhaps it was the second who perished at Camlann. However that may be, the Welsh told a story about the causes of the battle. It was centred on Arthur's residence in Cornwall, Kelliwic. Medraut raided it while Arthur was absent. His men ate all the food, leaving not so much as would feed a fly, and he dragged Guinevere from her chair and struck her, or worse. Arthur retaliated by raiding Medraut's abode. Those events led up to the murderous, much-bewailed battle which was fatal to both. Camlann was one of the 'futile' battles bracketed with Arfderydd where Merlin went mad.

It sounds like a mere barbaric feud. 'Kelliwic' means 'woodland' and it is not certain what place in Cornwall is meant, though the best candidate is another earthwork like Castle Dore, the half-obliterated Killibury or Kelly Rounds east of Wadebridge. As for 'Camlann' or 'Camlan', it is probably derived from a word in the British language, *Camboglanna*, 'crooked bank'— that is, of a winding river. North-west Wales has a Camlan or two to this day. They have nothing to do with Arthur, but they serve to show how indefinite the name is. There was a Roman fort called Camboglanna on Hadrian's Wall. It may have been Birdoswald, which has a winding river, the Irthing, below it in a valley. But Hadrian's Wall is a long way from Cornwall and cannot be brought into relation with any version of the catastrophe. By the way, as I mentioned before, the Somerset river Cam has been proposed also.

As if aware of this geographic dead end, Welsh story-tellers have shifted

Opposite above
St Govan's Chapel on the southern coast of Pembroke. Sir Gawain's grave is said to have been found somewhere near the sea-shore in this part of Wales during the reign of William the Conqueror; it has been claimed that 'St Govan' is actually Gawain, and that the knight's bones lie in a tomb under the chapel altar.

Opposite below
The pass near Snowdon where Arthur is said to have been felled by the arrows of Medraut's soldiers.

Birdoswald, a Roman fort in Cumbria, on Hadrian's Wall. It may be
the one recorded as Camboglanna. This name would have become
'Camlann' in Welsh, and Camboglanna, which certainly existed, has
been claimed as the scene of Arthur's last battle.

The River Irthing below the Birdoswald fort. Its winding course is
in keeping with the meaning of 'Camboglanna'—the Crooked Bank.

A view from Llanberis, Gwynedd, looking towards Snowdon. Among the mountains near here is Marchlyn Mawr, a lake where Arthurian treasure is said to be concealed; Snowdon itself has some further speculative associations with Arthur.

the battle about quite fancifully and, indeed, irresponsibly. One very circum-
stantial account looks to Snowdonia, its inspiration being the notion that
Camlann was really a valley among the mountains called Cwm-y-llan, not the
Crooked Bank at all. This version tells how Arthur set out with his army from
Dinas Emrys where Merlin met Vortigern, and marched to Cwm Tregalan
above Cwm-y-llan. Here he confronted the followers of Medraut. They withdrew towards the summit of Snowdon, and then into a pass. When Arthur
entered the pass they shot arrows at him and he fell. The pass is called Bwlch y
Saethau, the Pass of the Arrows, to this day. Arthur was buried there and a
heap of stones was piled over him, Carnedd Arthur, Arthur's Cairn, a mile or
so from the peak. I don't think this fantasy is very old, and I don't think it was
ever taken seriously—Arthur's Cairn has never been cited to refute the Glas-

The River Camel near Slaughter Bridge, Cornwall. This river is Geoffrey of
Monmouth's choice as the Camlann where Arthur fell fighting Mordred. He
may have picked the location because of reports of weapons and armour being
dug up in neighbouring fields, but if so, they were probably relics of a later
battle between the Saxons and Cornish.

tonbury grave—but it shows how Camlann could stir the imagination while totally losing touch with reality.

Geoffrey took up the tale of this clash, but he could not accept the scenario of two chiefs killing each other in a personal quarrel, with no conflict of good and evil. Probably seeing how vague the whole business was, he moulded it cheerfully to his own ends. Medraut became Modred, the King's traitorous nephew. If I am right about Riothamus, Geoffrey adapted Riothamus's betrayal by a deputy-ruler who intrigued with barbarians. Developing his fiction, he made out that Modred was Arthur's deputy during his absence in Gaul, and conspired with the Saxons to achieve royal power himself. Instead of going to Avallon in Burgundy, Geoffrey's Arthur returns to Britain and fights Modred. While Geoffrey discarded Kelliwic, he knew that the logic of

A stone slab 9½ feet long, now beside the Camel near Slaughter Bridge but formerly somewhere in the fields marking a grave. It bears an inscription naming the grave's occupant as Latinus son of Magarus. In the final Latin word MAGARI—'of Magarus', the letters after the M were once misread as ATRY and made out to be a corrupt form of ARTHUR—a far-fetched piece of wishful thinking.

the Welsh story called for a Camlann in Cornwall or not too far off, and he hit on the Cornish river Camel, where his Arthur, victorious but grievously wounded, departs to a more mysterious Avalon for healing. It is a very skilful literary creation.

Cornish legend prompted by Geoffrey identifies the site of Arthur's last battle as a field near Slaughter Bridge. This aptly named bridge spans the Camel about a mile above Camelford. The river flows along a small valley with trees overhanging it. Dead and dying men, it is said, tumbled into it in such numbers that it ran red with blood. Arthur and Modred fought on the bridge itself, hand to hand. Modred was slain, but his sword was poisoned, and Arthur, mortally wounded by it, walked a little way upstream and collapsed. An inscribed stone beside the river was once imagined to have his name on it, but only because of a highly wishful misreading, long since refuted. John Leland, the Tudor traveller who equates Cadbury with Camelot, speaks of fragments of armour and other military gear being dug up in the fields. These were probably relics of a battle in 823 between the Saxons and Cornish. Geoffrey may have been drawn to the Camel by reports of similar finds.

The romancers keep the dramatic motif of Modred's treachery and seizure of power, and his name undergoes a further change to 'Mordred', acquiring a

deathlike ring. The geography, however, flies off into new vagaries. A French writer places the final conflict on Salisbury Plain. Malory, more or less following him but moving away from the Plain itself, specifies 'a down beside Salisbury', not far from the sea. The 'sea' part is an unrealistic plot requirement, but the 'down' is workable. Could there have been some forgotten tale locating the battle on the famous hill of Old Sarum, the Sorviodunum of the Romans, close to the 'crooked bank' of the Avon?

Malory, anyhow, re-evokes the dreadful futility. Arthur is warned in a dream by Gawain's ghost. He tries to buy time by negotiating a treaty with Mordred. Neither trusts the other, and the officers in both armies are under orders to attack instantly if they see a sword drawn. The pact is agreed upon, but an adder slithers out of the bushes and stings a knight's foot. Without thinking, he draws his sword to kill it. Fighting breaks out and rages on till hardly anyone is left. Arthur personally kills Mordred, but is fatally wounded by him.

Tennyson, who did his homework more conscientiously than you might think, takes the battle back to Cornwall or, more precisely, to Lyonesse. Its locale in *The Passing of Arthur* is a sandy waste, meant, I think, to be what is now the sea-bed near Porthleven. Arthur has been pursuing Mordred, and catches up with him at the winter solstice, a time of symbolic gloom. The battle is a nightmare chaos in which the ideal monarchy simply disintegrates.

> Nor ever yet had Arthur fought a fight
> Like this last, dim, weird battle of the west.
> A deathwhite mist slept over sand and sea;
> Whereof the chill, to him who breathed it, drew
> Down with his blood, till all his heart was cold
> With formless fear; and ev'n on Arthur fell
> Confusion, since he saw not whom he fought.
> For friend and foe were shadows in the mist,
> And friend slew friend not knowing whom he slew;
> And some had visions out of golden youth,
> And some beheld the faces of old ghosts
> Look in upon the battle; and in the mist
> Was many a noble deed, many a base,
> And chance and craft and strength in single fights,
> And ever and anon with host to host
> Shocks, and the splintering spear, the hard mail hewn,
> Shield-breakings, and the clash of brands, the crash

Opposite
Salisbury Plain, Wiltshire, to which a medieval romancer transfers Arthur's last battle. A view from Stonehenge.

Old Sarum, the Roman Sorviodunum, a hill near Salisbury and the Wiltshire Avon, with ancient fortifications and remains of medieval buildings. The latter, of course, would not have been there in Arthur's time. Malory's allusion to a 'down beside Salisbury', rather than the actual Plain, as the scene of Arthur's last fatal encounter with Mordred, allows speculation about a possible legend of this famous hill.

Of battleaxes on shatter'd helms, and shrieks
After the Christ, of those who falling down
Look'd up for heaven, and only saw the mist;
And shouts of heathen and the traitor knights,
Oaths, insult, filth, and monstrous blasphemies,
Sweat, writhings, anguish, labouring of the lungs
In that close mist, and cryings for the light,
Moans of the dying, and voices of the dead.

The ultimate horror of the mist is a Tennysonian contribution which John Boorman adopted in the film *Excalibur*.

When all is hushed and the mist has dispersed, Bedivere carries the wounded King to a 'dark strait of barren land' with the sea on one side and a lake on the other. Tennyson has taken a hint from Loe Bar, a ridge of sand and pebbles which divides the sea from Loe Pool. However, he makes the ridge higher and more precipitous, and the lake larger and more mysterious, leading out of our world to an uncharted 'deep' which is the way to Avalon, or, as he spells it, Avilion. Arthur commands Bedivere to throw Excalibur into it and,

after twice disobeying, he does so. A hand rises from the water, catches the sword by its jewelled hilt, and draws it under. Then a barge approaches over the lake with a company of ladies, and they bear Arthur off.

Like the more mellifluous spelling of 'Avalon', this departure by water is taken from Malory, who himself takes it from an older romance. The theme of the casting-away of Arthur's sword is also much older than Tennyson, and the incident, like the battle, is claimed by several places. Romantic fancy points not only to Loe Pool but to Dozmary Pool, a great tarn on Bodmin Moor surrounded by open grassland and bare hills. You reach it by turning off the A30 at the celebrated Jamaica Inn. In winter Dozmary Pool can look eerie, with mist hiding its farther shore, and local legend used to assert that it was bottomless, till it dried up in 1859 and was revealed to be quite shallow.

Oddly, both Loe Pool and Dozmary Pool have authentic folklore connections, but with someone other than Arthur, namely Jan Tregeagle (pronounced Tregayle), a cruel seventeenth-century magistrate who became a Cornish arch-villain. His ghost was condemned to toil at impossible tasks. One was to empty Dozmary Pool with a leaky limpet shell. Another was to move all the sand from Berepper to Porthleven, across what was then the open mouth of Loe Pool. He carried sackload after sackload, but the tide kept sweeping it back, building up Loe Bar. The Bar was completed when Tregeagle, tripped by a demon, spilt the sack he was carrying.

At Glastonbury, the claim to Arthur's grave produced a claim to another resting-place for Excalibur. Bedivere flung it into the mere at Pomparles Bridge—*pont périlleux*, the perilous bridge—across the Brue near the end of Wearyall Hill. In Arthur's day there would at least have been a mere.

While the Excalibur story is a work of imagination, it may be based on an actual custom. Swords have been found in Denmark under ancient lakes turned into peat-bogs, and they were carefully laid there, sometimes deliberately bent, in fenced-off areas. A warrior's sword was peculiarly his own, an extension of himself, and swords may have been sunk in water after the owner's death to prevent anyone else from using them.

One way or another, Arthur departed from mortal life. However, the two people closest to him were still living. Guinevere had been caught in Mordred's rebellion. Geoffrey of Monmouth, who knows nothing of Lancelot, says she joined briefly in the betrayal and accepted the traitor as her lover. Malory, for whom the Queen is far more important and far more sympathetic, says she only pretended to fall in with his plans, and shut herself in the Tower of London out of his reach. Both authors agree that she entered a

Opposite
Old Sarum. A small part of the interior, where the amount of open space
might encourage imagination to conjure up a battle.

Loe Bar, Cornwall, with Loe Pool in the foreground. The Pool is the largest lake in Cornwall, running inland towards Helston. It was once an inlet of the sea but the formation of the Bar closed it off, supplying Tennyson, centuries after, with an idea for his portrayal of Arthur's Passing.

Dozmary Pool, on Bodmin Moor about 900 feet above sea-level. Across it are the Brown Gelly Downs, populated in prehistoric times. Its Excalibur story may be quite recent, and does not fit in well with other Arthurian geographic ideas.

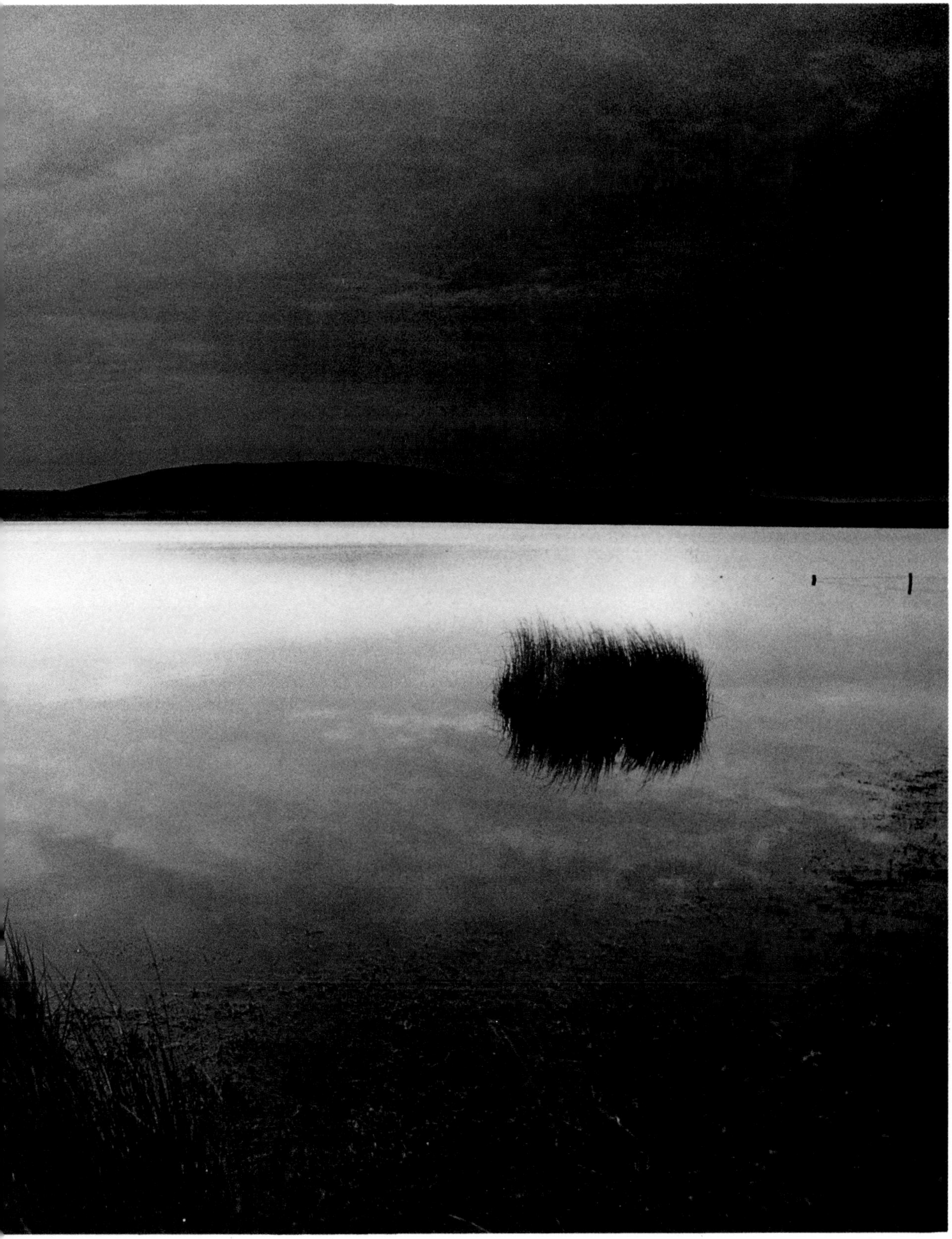

convent, Malory says at Amesbury, which lies below the eastern rim of Salisbury Plain. A monastery may have been here before the Saxons, in a bend of the Avon near the present church of Saints Mary and Melor. Amesbury had a women's community too, perhaps not early enough for Guinevere, but that is where Malory pictures her.

Knowing that her amour with Lancelot had led to divided loyalties and, in the end, to an outright breach which Mordred exploited, she devoted herself to penitence and charity. Meanwhile Lancelot had been living in France, estranged, ruling over lands of his own with many knights formerly loyal to Arthur. On receiving news of Mordred's revolt he hurried back to aid the King, but too late. It was all over, and he rode westwards grief-stricken to find Guinevere. As he walked into the Amesbury cloister she saw him first, and asked her ladies to fetch him. She was free at last of evasion and self-deception.

When Sir Lancelot was brought to her, then she said to all the ladies, 'Through this man and me hath all this war been wrought, and the death of the most noblest knights of the world; for through our love that we have loved together is my most noble lord slain. Therefore, Sir Lancelot, wit thou well I am set in such a plight to get my soul health; and yet I trust through God's grace that after my death to have a sight of the blessed face

of Christ, and at doomsday to sit on his right side, for as sinful as ever I was are saints in heaven. Therefore, Sir Lancelot, I require thee and beseech thee heartily, for all the love that ever was betwixt us, that thou never see me more in the visage... for as well as I have loved thee, mine heart will not serve me to see thee, for through thee and me is the flower of kings and knights destroyed; therefore, Sir Lancelot, go to thy realm, and there take thee a wife, and live with her in joy and bliss.'

No, he answered, he could never do that.

'I take record of God, in you I have had mine earthly joy; and if I had founden you now so disposed, I had cast me to have had you into mine own realm.'

But as she would not accompany him, he too would renounce the world. He would kiss her once and take his leave. Not even once, she replied. He must go.

And they departed. But there was never so hard an hearted man but he would have wept to see the dolour that they made.

Lancelot settled as a hermit with other survivors in a little valley near Glastonbury, doubtless the valley of Chalice Well at the foot of the Tor. When Guinevere died he brought her body to Glastonbury for burial, and then pined away till he died himself, and they took him to Joyous Gard and the tomb prepared for him.

Opposite
Amesbury, Wiltshire. Near this peaceful spot by the Avon a religious community may have existed before the Saxon conquest. There was certainly a convent in later times. Malory tells of Guinevere retiring here in the final catastrophe, and saying farewell to Lancelot when he comes to look for her.

7. Arthur's Destiny

WHAT, FINALLY, HAPPENED TO THE KING?
An old Welsh poem says his grave is a mystery. If the Glastonbury monks spoke truly, the secret was known to some and was disclosed to Henry II. Malory wavers. Perhaps Arthur was indeed buried at Glastonbury, perhaps Guinevere was indeed laid beside him. Though the ladies took him away in their boat, he died almost at once, and they disembarked and bore his corpse into central Somerset, the Vale of Avilion. Yet as Malory puts it, 'some men say in many parts of England that King Arthur is not dead, but had by the will of Our Lord Jesu into another place; and men say that he shall come again.'

Even the Abbey grave, seemingly so conclusive, has been given a supernatural glamour. According to one tale, when Arthur received his fatal wound he was carried back to his birthplace at Tintagel and died there, and the wind and sea made uncanny noises around the headland till the body was taken on to Glastonbury and laid in the ground. In Malory's time Arthur's remains had been transferred to the black marble tomb before the high altar, and Malory quotes an inscription stated to be on it calling Arthur REX QUONDAM REXQUE FUTURUS, 'King that was, and King that shall be.' He will return.

As for Avalon, if it is not Glastonbury, it is simply a magical retreat where Arthur lives on. Geoffrey, in his *Life of Merlin*, imagines the 'apple-island' as somewhere over vague waters, a Fortunate Isle of natural plenty and longevity, the home of kindly enchantresses. Some romancers, more daring, shift

Opposite
King Arthur's Cave, on the edge of the Forest of Dean, a few miles north-east of Monmouth. People lived in it in the Stone Age. Close by is the hill-fort Little Doward where Geoffrey of Monmouth locates the death of Vortigern, but the reason for the cave's connection with Arthur himself is uncertain.

it to the Mediterranean. Tennyson has the barge carrying Arthur set its course for an Otherworld beyond the mere:

'I am going a long way
With these thou seest—if indeed I go
(For all my mind is clouded with a doubt)—
To the island-valley of Avilion;
Where falls not hail, or rain, or any snow,
Nor ever wind blows loudly; but it lies
Deep-meadow'd, happy, fair with orchard lawns
And bowery hollows crown'd with summer sea,
Where I will heal me of my grievous wound.'

This is the literary legend. The folk-legend is something else again. A popular notion of Arthur's immortality may have begun in Brittany, where a people of British stock cherished their own beliefs about him. It was certainly well-established in Cornwall by 1113, when some French priests visiting Bodmin, assured by locals that Arthur was still alive, laughed at them and were startled to find that they had a fight on their hands. In Wales and farther north Arthur sleeps in a cave as he does at Cadbury, and so do many of his knights, and with them is his royal treasure. Some day he will wake and restore justice and peace throughout the land. As I mentioned earlier, the folklorist Jennifer Westwood sees this legend as evidence that Arthur existed. Similar stories are told of heroes in several countries, and in every known case or virtually so the sleeper is a historical person. While the remote inspiration of the motif is likely to be mythical, the mortals on whom it fastens are not gods or fairy-tale figures but real humans. The argument holds even though Arthur's cave-legend in various forms is widely spread, with fifteen or more locations.

Few versions relate to an actual cave. Usually the cave is a mysterious recess like the one at Cadbury, which no one finds or enters except under special circumstances. Of the two or three 'Arthur's Caves' that do exist, the most important is on the fringes of the Forest of Dean. A small road leaves the A40 at Ganarew near the hill-fort Little Doward, the scene of the death of Vortigern. After sundry twistings and turnings you reach the top of a path leading down, across the valley from the hill-fort. It passes a quarry and goes on to the cave, in a beech wood. This has a serious, non-legendary interest as

Opposite
Craig-y-Ddinas, Mid Glamorgan. Somewhere here, supposedly, a well-hidden tunnel goes down to a subterranean chamber where Arthur and his knights lie sleeping, till the day dawns for them to restore justice and peace throughout Britain. A visitor, guided by a magician, was allowed to carry off some gold from a treasure-hoard, but met with disaster when he came back for more.

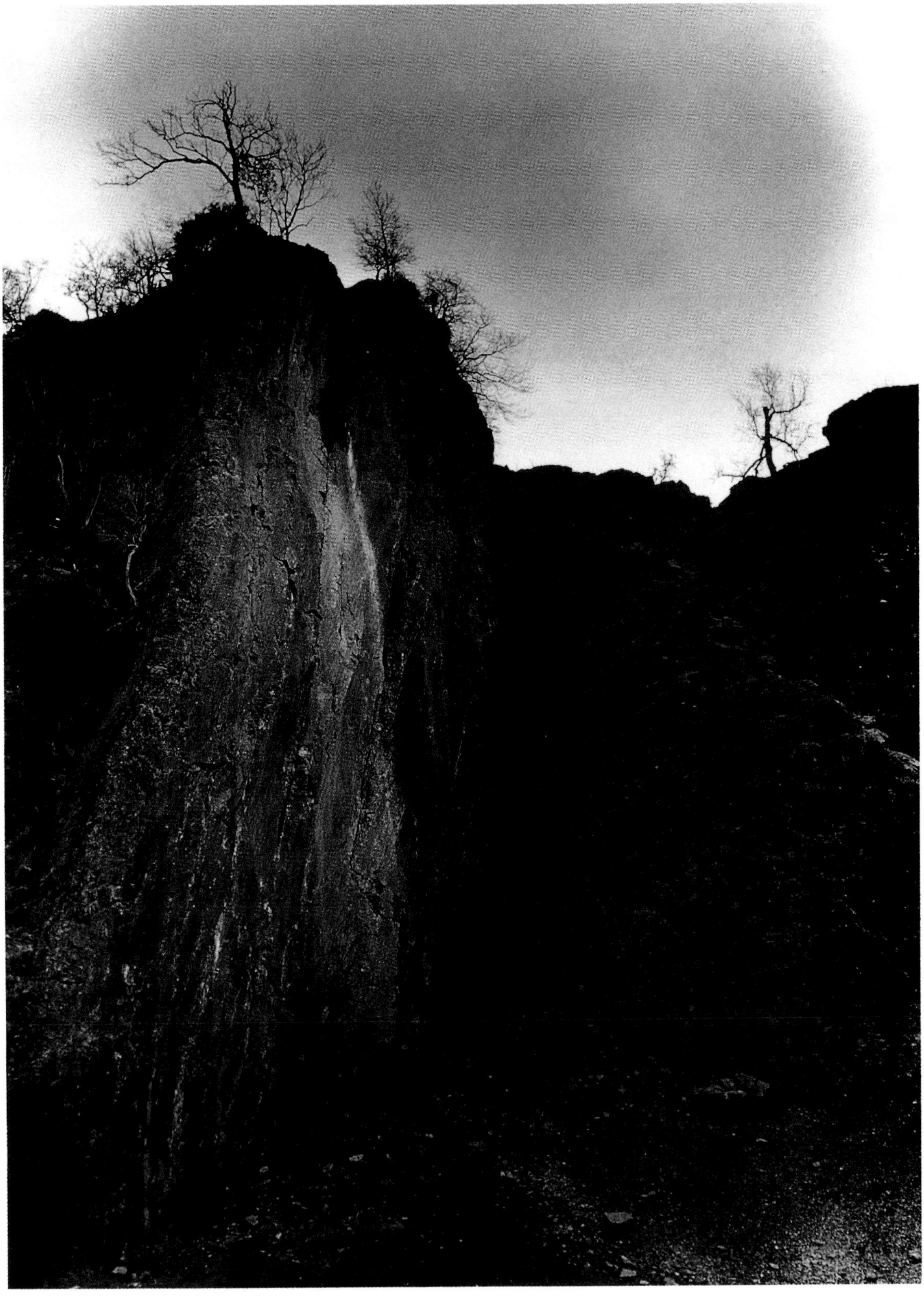

the dwelling of Stone Age people ten thousand years ago, and of others intermittently since. It does not penetrate far into the hillside, but its innermost chamber is cut off from daylight and the visitor should bring a torch. The nearby presence of Vortigern, and of Arthur's uncle who besieged him, may have suggested Arthur himself; but I am not sure what his connection with the cave is supposed to be, though I have heard that it *is* one of those where he lies asleep . . . presumably in a deeper chamber with a blocked or concealed entry.

In the legendary cases where someone finds him, or his knights, the experience may involve a kind of test or ordeal and is apt to be alarming. Craig-y-Ddinas in Glamorgan, the 'Rock of the Fortress', rises steeply at the head of the Vale of Neath, above the confluence of two rivers. It is said to have been one of the last haunts in Wales of the fairy-folk. Once upon a time a Welshman was crossing London Bridge carrying a staff of hazel wood. An Englishman, soon revealed to be a magician, told him that if they went to the place where it had been cut, he could be rich. The Welshman took him to Craig-y-Ddinas and pointed out the stump of the tree. Under it was a flat stone, and when they lifted the stone, a passage appeared leading downwards. A bell hung from the roof. They descended to a vast cavern where warriors in armour lay asleep in a circle. Arthur, their chief, had a golden crown beside him. Inside the circle were a heap of gold and a heap of silver. The wizard said his companion was free to take what he could carry from one heap or the other, but must be careful not to touch the bell on the way up. If he did, one of the knights would wake and ask if it was day, and then the only means of escape was to reply 'No, sleep on.'

The Welshman loaded himself with so much gold that as they retraced their steps, he walked clumsily and hit the bell. It rang, a knight started up with the question, he gave the answer, and the knight went to sleep again. They replaced the slab and the stump, and the wizard left, with a warning not to squander the gold. However, the Welshman did squander it, and returned for more. Again he rang the bell, and this time he had forgotten the answer. More of the warriors awoke, took back the gold, gave him a beating, and ejected him. Henceforth he was poor and infirm, and could never find the cave again.

Opposite
Alderley Edge, Cheshire. The outcrop where water drips into a stone trough, which counts as a wishing well. A face is carved on the rock above, perhaps representing Merlin, who figures in the local version of the Arthurian cave-legend.

Here the visitor is put through a test of character. In some places it is more like a test of nerve. Alderley Edge in Cheshire is the wooded north face of a sandstone ridge above the town of the same name. A path runs along it to a spot where water drips from a rocky outcrop into a stone trough. Above on the rock is a carved, weathered face which is alleged to represent Merlin, and an inscription: DRINK OF THIS AND TAKE THY FILL FOR THE WATER FALLS BY THE WIZARDS WILL. The inscription is not old, the face may be. Merlin, according to the story, met a farmer on his way to Macclesfield market with a white mare which he hoped to sell. The magician offered to buy her. The farmer thought the price too low and went on, but was unable to find a purchaser. On the way back Merlin stopped him again, saying he had a better offer, and led him to a rock on Alderley Edge which opened, disclosing a pair of gates. They passed through into a cave. Merlin explained that Arthur and his knights were asleep here till their country needed them. 'They have horses with them,' he continued, 'but they still need another white one. Will you sell?' He held out a purse of gold and the farmer took it, but the uncanniness of the situation overwhelmed him, and he rushed out in a panic. The gates shut, the rock closed, and no one ever found the place afterwards.

In this case the visitor at least gets his gold and survives intact. At Richmond in Yorkshire he is less fortunate. Richmond Castle stands on a height above the Swale. Castle Walk runs along the hillside below, not unlike the path along Alderley Edge. Among the woods a potter named Thompson stumbled on the mouth of a tunnel. He walked in and reached a chamber where Arthur and several knights were sitting asleep at a round table, with a sword and a horn on it. Thompson touched the sword, or picked up the horn, or both (accounts differ), whereupon the sleepers began stirring. Terrified, he ran back along the tunnel, and heard a voice calling after him:

> Potter Thompson, Potter Thompson!
> If thou hadst drawn the sword or blown the horn,
> Thou hadst been the luckiest man e'er born.

It was too late.

The Alderley Edge and Richmond themes come together in the legend of the Eildon Hills near Melrose recorded by Sir Walter Scott, who lived at Abbotsford three or four miles away. They are three peaks close beside the town, traversed by the Eildon Walk. It climbs over heather and gorse and

Opposite
Alderley Edge. The face on the rock—Merlin?—above the wishing well.
Under it the roughly carved letters say: DRINK OF THIS AND TAKE THY
FILL FOR THE WATER FALLS BY THE WIZARDS WILL.

Richmond Castle, North Yorkshire. Another locale of the cave legend. Among the woods below the castle, dropping away to the Swale, a potter named Thompson finds an underground passage leading into a cavern. Arthur and several knights are sitting at a round table, asleep. In this case the story of the King may have been super-imposed on an older legend which tells only of the passage, alleging that it leads to Easby Abbey a mile away, and is haunted by the ghost of an army drummer-boy who rashly explored it.

The Eildon Hills, near Melrose in Scotland. Sir Walter Scott tells a Border legend of the poet and seer Thomas the Rhymer taking a horse-dealer into a cave under the highest of the hills, and showing him Arthur's knights asleep.

patches of red soil, passes between the northern and central summits, and swings right to descend on the west opposite Bowden Moor. There, low down between the central and southernmost of the hills, is an incongruous rocky hillock, the Lucken Hare, once a gathering-place of witches.

One night, so Scott relates, a horse-dealer named Canonbie Dick was going home with two unsold horses. On Bowden Moor he met a stranger in antiquated clothing, who bought the horses, paying for them with obsolete coins, which, however, were of gold and therefore acceptable. The same thing happened several times. Dick asked the stranger where he lived, and he agreed to take him there, but warned that if he showed any fear he would suffer for it.

The stranger was the thirteenth-century poet and seer Thomas of Ercel-doune, Thomas the Rhymer, reputed to have foretold the Battle of Bannock-burn and the accession of James I when the burn flowed past Merlin's grave, and to have dwelt seven years in Elfland with its queen. Well versed in the mysteries of these hills, he led Dick to the Lucken Hare, and through a hidden door into an immense torchlit space under the highest peak, the Eildon Tree. Armoured knights lay slumbering, with horses beside them. At the far end was a table, and on it were a sword and a horn. Thomas told Dick to draw the sword and blow the horn. It must be his own decision which to do first. If he made the right choice he would be 'king of all Britain'. This promise is not clear; perhaps it meant that he would be a precursor or deputy of Arthur, before the restoration of the King himself. Dick reflected, and decided that drawing the sword might look aggressive, so he blew the horn. With a thunderous din the knights started to move. Understandably, Dick did show the fear he had been warned against, and a voice informed him that he had shown it already by his choice. Drawing the sword would have been the act of a warrior; blowing the horn was the act of a man summoning help.

> Woe to the coward, that ever he was born,
> Who did not draw the sword before he blew the horn!

A mighty wind swept him out of the cave and the door slammed behind him. He told some shepherds what had happened, and fell dead. The Lucken Hare keeps its secret.

Nobody knows how old such stories are, but the spread of Arthur's re-nown is real enough. One way or another, he is associated with fully 150 places, from the Isles of Scilly far into Scotland. No other character is so widespread in Britain except the Devil. Significantly, though, the spread is not even. Most of the Arthur locations are in areas where Celtic people kept their identity longest, and sometimes keep it still—the West Country, especially Cornwall; Wales; northern England; southern Scotland. Despite his national fame in romance, Arthur has never rooted himself in the more English ter-ritories, Anglo-Saxondom. As a hero of folklore and a presence on the map,

Hadrian's Wall in
Northumberland, running
along the top of a series of
crags. In the open country
beyond this point, to the left,
are King's Crags and
Queen's Crags where Arthur
and Guinevere, pictured in
folklore as giants, sit and
quarrel at long range.

Dozmary Pool, on Bodmin
Moor in Cornwall. One of
several places with a story of
the casting away of Excalibur
into the water.

Loe Bar, Cornwall, a ridge of sand and pebbles dividing Loe Pool (in the foreground) from the sea. Tennyson, in his poetic version of the Passing of Arthur, imagines a 'dark strait of barren land', where Sir Bedivere takes the wounded King after his last battle and helps him to the barge that bears him away. The imagery was suggested by this ridge.

he belongs almost wholly to regions where his saga took shape and Celtic story-tellers recalled his deeds, before Geoffrey made literature of them. Even London has only one legend bringing Arthur there which goes back beyond medieval fancy. (It concerns Tower Hill, where the head of the prehistoric king Bran was buried as a talisman against foreign plagues and invasions, and Arthur unwisely dug it up on the ground that Britain should not rely on such things.)

There is no saying when or where the saga began. People were apparently naming their sons 'Arthur' at least as early as the latter half of the sixth century. About the same time, Cumbrian bards were composing the first poetry in Welsh, and verses ascribed to one of them, Aneirin, mention Arthur as proverbial for prowess in battle. The poem is one of a long series of elegies entitled *Gododdin*, commemorating a force of Britons who assembled near Edinburgh, marched south against the Angles, and fell fighting them at Catterick in Yorkshire, towards the year 600. Seemingly they attacked the Roman fort near the strategic road junction now called Scotch Corner. It stood by the south bank of the Swale at Catterick Bridge. One of the poems priases a warrior named Gwawrddur for his success in 'glutting black ravens on the wall of the fort, though he was not Arthur'. In early Welsh poetic language, feeding the ravens meant killing enemies, making carrion of them. The point of the lines is that Gwawrddur was a terrific raven-feeder even though he wasn't the greatest of all. If they are truly part of Aneirin's original, they attest Arthur's pre-eminence in heroic tradition about 600. They may have been added later, but even so they still attest his pre-eminence at whatever time they were added, and it was certainly long before Geoffrey. Likewise do early things from Wales which we have glanced at—the history by 'Nennius', the *Annales Cambriae*—and others which we have not.

Occasionally the Arthur of folk-memory is more than human. He can sound like some primordial titan. Walking through Carmarthenshire, he felt a pebble in his shoe, and took it out and tossed it away. It flew seven miles through the air and dropped to earth in the Gower peninsula on top of some smaller stones. The cluster is still there on Cefn Bryn Common, a fragmentary megalith, and the stone on top—the one from the shoe—is called Arthur's Stone and weighs 25 tons. Up in Northumberland, in the broad sweep of open

Opposite above
Brecon Beacons in Powys, Wales, as seen looking along the ridge where
Arthur, according to Welsh legend, assembled the followers who became the
Knights of the Round Table.

Opposite below
Brecon Beacons. The dip between the two peaks, Pen y Fan and Corn Du, has long been
known as Arthur's Chair. The lake in the foreground is Llyn Cwm Llwch. Somewhere in it
there is said to be an invisible island of fairy-folk which mortals used to be able to reach on
May Day, when a doorway near the shore opened into a tunnel. But one visitor took a
flower back with him, and the door closed for ever.

The Eildon Hills. The hillock is the Lucken Hare where, in Scott's version of the cave-legend, Thomas leads the horse-dealer underground through a secret door. Witches used to gather here.

Craig Arthur, 'Arthur's Rock', in Clwyd. One of the various natural features with Arthur's name attached to them. Craig Arthur forms the end of a massive ridge of exposed strata, running northwards from Dinas Bran above Llangollen.

Above
Arthur's Quoit in Anglesey, one of at least eleven stones so called. Most are in
Wales, where the Welsh name is Coetan Arthur. This one is the capstone of the
Lligwy dolmen, a prehistoric burial chamber.

Opposite
The Swale near Catterick Bridge, North Yorkshire. A Roman fort here is
generally assumed to be the strong-point called Catraeth in the Welsh poem-
cycle *Gododdin*, telling of a brave but futile attack by a British force on the
northern Angles, about the close of the sixth century. One line glances at
Arthur as proverbial for prowess in war.

Arthur's Seat east of Edinburgh, the best known of four natural formations so named. The remnant of an extinct volcano, it rises 823 feet above sea-level. While traces of early defensive works may be significant, the main reason for the name is presumably a dip between two high points, giving the same effect as Arthur's Chair in the Brecon Beacons.

country north-west of Sewingshields on Hadrian's Wall, are two sandstone outcrops half a mile apart. These are King's Crags and Queen's Crags. On King's Crags is a natural formation called Arthur's Chair. Once when Arthur quarrelled with Guinevere, he sat in this chair while she sat aloof on Queen's Crags, and tossed a boulder at her. It hit her comb and fell in the space between, where it still lies, bearing the toothmarks of the comb.

King's Crags is not the only place where a colossal Arthur sits. From Edinburgh you see Arthur's Seat to the eastward, an extinct volcano more than eight hundred feet high, with the Palace of Holyroodhouse at its foot. It has remains of defensive works that may go back to the day when the warriors in *Gododdin* gathered to prepare their campaign. But the 'Arthur's Seat' idea is suggested by a dip between two high points, providing a kind of saddle suitable for a giant. Edinburgh's fame has diverted attention from three other Arthur's Seats. One is Dumbarrow Hill near Letham in Tayside, which also has two tops with a dip between, and is in a part of Scotland with legends of Arthur and Mordred. The other Arthur's Seats are on the mountain Ben Arthur to the west of Loch Long, and a Cumbrian hill east of Liddesdale.

Wales has a comparable site on the Brecon Beacons, where the space between the two highest points, Corn Du and Pen y Fan, has been known as Arthur's Chair since at least the twelfth century. In this case a more mundane imagination has reacted against the fantasy, and a legend reduces Arthur to human stature by explaining that he set his throne on this height when he summoned his court to form the Round Table knighthood. It seems a bleak place for such a ceremony but, the legend adds, the proof is that boulders scattered round Pen y Fan are pieces of the Table itself.

8. The Enduring Theme

To FOLLOW ARTHUR about the country, and in literature, is to realize what a shape-shifter he is. He has been so very different at different times and in different settings. The Welsh made him the central figure of a Celtic heroic age, an age of warriors and saints and monsters and marvels, as in the tale *Culhwch and Olwen*. Geoffrey of Monmouth made him a great ruler and conqueror, a virtual emperor, with a realm challenging the glories of historical empires and supplying a precedent for the claims of the Norman kings. The romancers turned Arthur's Britain into a chivalric Utopia, with gallant knights riding out on quests and engaging in courtly love-affairs. Tennyson took up this fanciful ideal kingdom and infused Victorian values. Modern novelists, aware that any real Arthur would probably have spent most of his time struggling against the forces of chaos and barbarism, have pictured him as a champion of Order, noble but doomed.

Yet a constant motif runs through all the versions. Even satirists who deride it, sometimes trenchantly, acknowledge its persistence by doing so. Each wave of story-telling is an attempt to substantiate an ancient dream, the dream of a long-lost Golden Age, in whatever guise and to whatever extent the story-tellers evoke it. At one extreme, the Golden Age may be pictured as a reign of prosperity and justice; at the other, merely as a phase when a few of the best and bravest were—though briefly, though hopelessly—in charge of events. The dream abides. That is a main reason for Arthur's continuing fascination. And the Golden Age in this British form has a special source of power, the prophecy of Arthur's return. The lost glory is not truly lost. Somehow its creator is still 'there', so to speak, and in the hour of need he will wake from sleep or come back from his island, to save his country and bring in the Golden Age again. The Glastonbury prophecy, with its foreshadowing of 'peace and plenty' when the Abbey revives, is not unrelated. No, we don't believe in a literal return of Arthur. Yet the symbolism of the myth is potent in its appeal, and perennial.

Where should this journey draw to a close? Because Arthur appears in so many places, he may seem to take leave of reality entirely, to be impossible to anchor at all. That, of course, is not an argument against his existence. A saga of him could have spread anywhere, and for that matter, a real Arthur could have gone anywhere, in the course of his wars and other activities. I would accept, though, that the literary clues in Britain cannot pin him down by themselves.

A number of scholars have claimed to find a key in the frequent occurrence of northern characters, northern themes, northern legends, and signs that some of these are early. They argue that Arthur's saga began in the north and was carried southwards to Wales and elsewhere; from which it is inferred that if a real Arthur existed he was a northerner. But this bias may only reflect the fact—and a fact it is—that the founders of Welsh literature were northern bards, such as Taliesin and Aneirin. They and their followers could have handed down northern traditions that flowed into the saga of an earlier, southern hero. It seems to me that even the oldest material of this type is not passing on history but early layers of legend. Moreover, the north never gives Arthur the firm roots which the West Country gives him. It has no equivalent for Tintagel, Cadbury or Glastonbury. It never gives him a birthplace, a headquarters or a grave, never pictures him as belonging in its territory. Nor, by the way, does early story-telling in Wales, however much Wales may claim Arthur as its own. The Welsh themselves put him in Cornwall and Somerset.

That alone would still prove little. But here archaeology comes in. We know now that in all three of those places in the West Country, the legend-weavers scored bull's-eyes. Tintagel *was* an inhabited centre, probably an important one, at about the right time. So was Glastonbury, where there *was* a fort (or something) on top of the Tor, and there *was* a grave. Neither at Tintagel nor at Glastonbury was there anything on the surface, when the stories were first told, to suggest them. As for Cadbury, it is surely decisive. It is no myth, it is a huge and palpable fact. But in 1542, when Leland said it was Camelot, he had no way of guessing at what it harboured. It was modern excavation, using techniques Leland could never have dreamed of, that showed it to be—as I said before—the only credible Camelot in the only credible sense.

In all three cases the Arthur connection has been dismissed as a late and groundless invention. Yet in all three cases, with nothing visible to guide it, the 'invention' focused on an appropriate site, chronologically correct. One such lucky guess would be possible, three is too much. The conclusion is inescapable. The West Country Arthur connection is based on historical tradition, reaching back all the way to the required period. Nothing to match that triple score can be produced in the north, and the Welsh legend of Dinas

Emrys, though alike in its implications, is not concerned with Arthur. I do not claim that the West Country stories are true, literally. I do claim that they are deeply rooted in some kind of reality. If I am right about Riothamus as the primary Arthur-figure, he clinches the matter.

So, I return. The beginning and end of the Arthurian Legend are both definite. For practical purposes Arthur has only the one starting-point, at Tintagel, and only the one grave, at Glastonbury. Whatever the truth about Tintagel, the solid reality of Cadbury-Camelot supports the belief in a great king in this part of England, and as for Glastonbury . . . well, there was certainly a grave. The journey may close where it began, in the presence of the Tor, and the Abbey, and that enigmatic spot where the bones came out of the earth, and the site of the tomb where they finally reposed: the tomb with the inscription which Malory quotes, if not as it was, yet surely as it ought to have been.

HIC IACET ARTHURUS, REX QUONDAM REXQUE FUTURUS
Here lies Arthur, King that was, and King that shall be

Principal Places and Natural Features

Alderley Edge
Alnwick
Amesbury
Anglesey
Arfderydd (= Arthuret)
Arthur's Cave
Arthur's Seat (four hills so named)
Avalon

Badbury Rings
Badon, Mount
Bamburgh
Bardsey Island
Bath
Bodmin
Brecon Beacons
Brent Knoll
Brittany

Cadbury Castle
Caerleon
Caledonian Wood (= Forest of
    Celidon)
Cam, River
Camboglanna (= Birdoswald?)
Camel, River
Camelford
Camelot
Camlann

Carlisle
Carmarthen
Castle Dore
Catterick
Celidon, Forest of (= Caledonian
    Wood)
Chester
City of the Legion
    (= Chester)
Cornwall
Craig Arthur
Craig-y-Ddinas
Cumbria

Dean, Forest of
Derwent Water
Devon
Dimilioc (= St Dennis?)
Dinas Emrys
Dinas Powys
Dozmary Pool
Drumelzier
Dumbarton
Dumnonia
Dunster
Dynevor

Edinburgh
Eildon Hills

Fowey

Glastonbury
Glein, River (=Glen?)
Gower
Great Arthur

Kelliwic (=Killibury?)
Kilmarth
King's Crags

Lancien (=Lantyan)
Liddington Castle
Lincolnshire
Linnuis (=Lindsey?)
Little Doward
Llancarfan
Llangollen
Loe Bar
London
Lothian
Lyonesse

Marazion
Marchlyn Mawr
Merlin's Cave
Monmouth
Mote of Mark
Mousehole

Nant Gwynant

Old Sarum

Penrith
Prescelly Mountains

Queen's Crags

Richmond

St Dennis
St Govan's Head
Salisbury Plain
Scilly, Isles of
Slaughter Bridge
Snowdonia
Somerset
Stirling
Stonehenge
Strathclyde

Tintagel
Tweed, River

Valle Crucis

Winchester
Wirral

Please refer to index for page references.

Bibliography

ALCOCK, LESLIE, *Arthur's Britain*. Allen Lane, the Penguin Press, 1971.

ALCOCK, LESLIE, *'By South Cadbury is that Camelot...'* (short title, *Cadbury-Camelot*). Thames and Hudson, 1972.

ALCOCK, LESLIE, 'Cadbury-Camelot: a Fifteen-Year Perspective', in *Proceedings of the British Academy* 68 (1982).

ASHE, GEOFFREY, *Avalonian Quest*. Methuen, 1982, and Collins, Fontana, 1984.

ASHE, GEOFFREY, 'A Certain Very Ancient Book', in *Speculum*, April 1981. The Medieval Academy of America, Cambridge, Massachusetts.

ASHE, GEOFFREY, *The Discovery of King Arthur*. Debrett, 1985; Doubleday, New York, 1985; Henry Holt, New York, 1987.

ASHE, GEOFFREY, *The Glastonbury Tor Maze*. Gothic Image, Glastonbury, 1979, and revised edition, 1985.

ASHE, GEOFFREY, *A Guidebook to Arthurian Britain*. Longman, 1980, and Aquarian Press (with additional matter), 1983.

ASHE, GEOFFREY, (ed.), *The Quest for Arthur's Britain*. Pall Mall, 1968; Paladin, 1971 and (with additional matter) 1982.

BROMWICH, RACHEL, *Trioedd Ynys Prydein*. The Welsh Triads, with translation and notes. University of Wales Press, Cardiff, 1961.

CAMPBELL, JAMES (ed.), *The Anglo-Saxons*. Phaidon, Oxford, 1982; Cornell University Press, Ithaca, N.Y., 1982.

CAVENDISH, RICHARD, *King Arthur and the Grail*. Weidenfeld and Nicolson, 1978.

CHAMBERS, E.K., *Arthur of Britain*. Sidgwick and Jackson, 1927, and re-issue, 1966.

DITMAS, E.M.R., *Tristan and Iseult in Cornwall*. Forrester Roberts, Gloucester, 1969.

DUMVILLE, DAVID, 'Sub-Roman Britain: History and Legend', in *History* 62 (1977).

GEOFFREY OF MONMOUTH, *Historia Regum Britanniae*. Latin text edited by Neil Wright. D.S. Brewer, Cambridge, 1985.

GEOFFREY OF MONMOUTH, *The History of the Kings of Britain*, translated, with introduction, by Lewis Thorpe. Penguin, 1966.

GEOFFREY OF MONMOUTH, *Vita Merlini* (The Life of Merlin), edited and translated by J.J. Parry. University of Illinois Press, Urbana, 1925.

GILDAS, *De Excidio Britanniae*, edited and translated under the title *The Ruin of Britain* by Michael Winterbottom, in *History from the Sources*, vol. 7. Phillimore, Chichester, 1978.

JOHN OF GLASTONBURY, *The Chronicle of Glastonbury Abbey*, edited by James P. Carley and translated by David Townsend. The Boydell Press, Woodbridge, 1985.

LACY, NORRIS J. (ed.), *The Arthurian Encyclopedia*. Garland, New York, 1986.

LAGORIO, VALERIE M., 'The Evolving Legend of St Joseph of Glastonbury', in *Speculum*, April 1971. The Medieval Academy of America, Cambridge, Massachusetts.

LOOMIS, ROGER SHERMAN (ed.), *Arthurian Literature in the Middle Ages*. Oxford, Clarendon Press, 1959.

Mabinogion, The. Translated by Gwyn Jones and Thomas Jones. Dent, 1949.

MALORY, SIR THOMAS, *Le Morte d'Arthur*. Caxton's text with modernized spelling by Janet Cowan. Penguin, 1969.

MORRIS, JOHN, *The Age of Arthur*. Weidenfeld and Nicolson, 1973.

'NENNIUS', *Historia Brittonum*, edited and translated under the title *British History* by John Morris, in *History from the Sources*, vol. 8. Phillimore, Chichester, 1980.

Perlesvaus. Translated by Nigel Bryant. D.S. Brewer, Cambridge, 1978.

RADFORD, C.A. RALEGH, 'Glastonbury Abbey', in Ashe (ed.), *The Quest for Arthur's Britain*.

RADFORD, C.A. RALEGH, *Glastonbury Abbey*. Pitkin, 1976.

RAHTZ, PHILIP, 'Glastonbury Tor', in Ashe (ed.), *The Quest for Arthur's Britain*.

RAHTZ, PHILIP, *Invitation to Archaeology*. Basil Blackwell, Oxford, 1985.

ROBINSON, JOSEPH ARMITAGE, *Two Glastonbury Legends*. Cambridge University Press, 1926.

SCOTT, JOHN, *The Early History of Glastonbury*. Boydell and Brewer, Woodbridge, 1981.

Sir Gawain and the Green Knight. Translated by Brian Stone. Penguin, 1974.

TOLSTOY, NIKOLAI, *The Quest for Merlin*. Hamish Hamilton, 1985.

TREHARNE, R.F., *The Glastonbury Legends*. Cresset, 1967.

VICKERY, A.R., *The Holy Thorn of Glastonbury*. West Country Folklore Series No. 12, Toucan Press, Guernsey, 1979.

WESTWOOD, JENNIFER, *Albion: a Guide to Legendary Britain*. Granada, 1985.

WILHELM, JAMES J., and GROSS, LEILA ZAMUELIS (eds.), *The Romance of Arthur*. Garland, New York, 1984.

WILLIAM OF MALMESBURY, *The Acts of the Kings of the English*. Translated as *William of Malmesbury's Chronicle* by John Sharpe, revised by J.A. Giles. Bohn, 1847.

WOOD, IAN, 'The End of Roman Britain', in *Gildas: New Approaches*, eds. Michael Lapidge and David Dumville. The Boydell Press, Woodbridge, 1984.

Glastonbury Tor. Focus of many mysteries. Once a pagan sanctuary and
entrance to the underworld, then a Christian centre and place linked with
Arthur and Guinevere. Its strange ruined tower and terraced slopes still
dominate the landscape of central Somerset.

Index